Mrs. W. Kelly

The Legend of
Sleepy Hollow
& Other Tales

BY

Washington Irving

CORE CLASSICS™

SERIES EDITOR MICHAEL J. MARSHALL

ABRIDGED BY REBECCA BEALL BARNS

LIBRARY OF CONGRESS CATALOG CARD NUMBER: 98-73794

ISBN 1-890517-14-3 TRADE PAPERBACK

DESIGNED BY BILL WOMACK STUDIO

COVER ILLUSTRATION BY GB MACINTOSH

CORE KNOWLEDGE FOUNDATION
801 EAST HIGH STREET
CHARLOTTESVILLE, VIRGINIA 22902

http://www.coreknowledge.org

The Legend of
Sleepy Hollow
& Other Tales

BY

Washington Irving

TABLE OF CONTENTS

INTRODUCTION

Introduction

AT THE TIME OF THE AMERICAN REVOLUTION Europeans tended to think of America as rough and uncivilized. Washington Irving's short stories came as a surprise to them. Indeed, a great part of his fame in America rested on the fact that he was the first New World writer who Old World readers considered worth reading.

Short stories themselves were new, too, and Irving's tales showed what their possibilities were. His sketches, as he called them, were entertaining, not preachy, as other short pieces of that era tended to be. They had distinctive characters in vivid settings. When his classically clear style joined those elements, Irving's tales became polished and satisfying.

Irving was certain that humor is life's saving grace. In the preface to one of his books of tales, he said, "I have always had an opinion that much good might be done by keeping mankind in good humor with each other." He wrote for pleasure and to give pleasure, but not just for the sake of being funny. His comic sense is rooted in his understanding of life's strange truths and sometimes sad twists.

"The Legend of Sleepy Hollow" and "Rip Van Winkle" have been among Americans' favorite stories since the day they first appeared. They are based on older German folktales whose settings are shifted to the Hudson River Valley in the days of New York's Dutch settlers, who had a reputation for being superstitious and fond of practical jokes. In both stories, those times have the aura of legend attached to them. Irving saw that the revolution of 1776 ended more than colonial government. The new nation, young and energetic, shook off old ways, including some that Irving found comforting. So, in remembrance, he gave the newborn United States myths of its past.

In "The Legend of Sleepy Hollow," Ichabod Crane, a spindly Connecticut schoolmaster, and Brom Bones, a strapping young Dutch farmer, are rivals for the affections of a blossoming farm lass, Katrina Van Tassel. Ichabod loves her for the bounty of her father's barn. Brom loves her for her figure. Ichabod's plans for parlaying the Van Tassel farm into a new mansion on the western frontier contrasts with the fun-loving nature of Brom Bones and hints that Irving saw his new country as becoming too caught up with money and status.

"Rip Van Winkle" is a fantasy of escape from adult responsibility. Rip is an overgrown child who sleeps through the years when he should be mature and able to take of himself and others. Sometimes we do wish we could be irresponsible and the story imagines a magical way to put into the past duties that might be unpleasant. But as Rip sleeps his world passes away. Rip does not fear the strange little men he meets deep in the mountains, but he does get scared when the people in his hometown no longer know who he is.

There were surely days when Irving, who regretted that he had idled through much his youth, would have been happy to curl up in a cozy corner and let time and worry just pass by. But in his tales he tells us we must accept changes, even when we don't want them to happen.

E. D. HIRSCH, JR.
CHARLOTTESVILLE, VIRGINIA

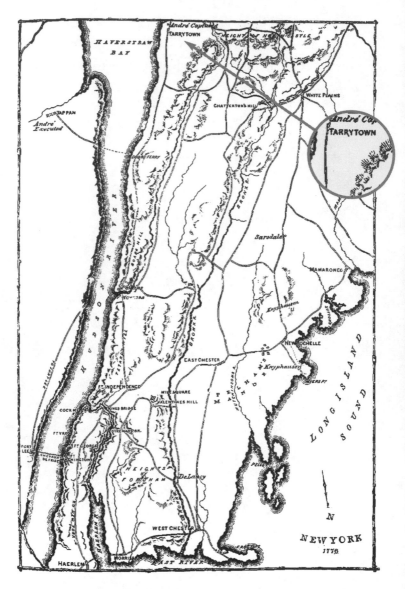

THE HUDSON RIVER VALLEY IN 1776

1

The Legend of Sleepy Hollow

IN ONE OF THOSE COVES ALONG THE EASTERN SHORE OF the Hudson, at that broad expanse of the river named by ancient Dutch navigators the Tappan Zee, lies a small rural port known by the name of Tarry Town. This name was given, we are told, by the housewives of the nearby country, from the habit of their husbands to linger about the village tavern on market days.

Not far from this village, about two miles away, is a little valley which is one of the quietest places in the world. A small brook glides through it with just murmur enough to lull one to sleep, and the whistle of a quail or tap of a woodpecker are almost the only sounds that ever break in upon the uniform tranquillity. There is no retreat from the world and its distractions more promising than this little valley.

From the stillness of the place, and the character of its inhabitants, who are descendants from the original Dutch settlers, this secluded glen has long been known by the name of Sleepy Hollow. A drowsy, dreamy influence seems to fill the very atmosphere. Some say that the place was bewitched during the early days of the settlement. Others say that an old Indian chief, the wizard of his tribe, held his pow-wows there before the country was discovered by **Henry Hudson**.

HENRY HUDSON
An English explorer hired by the Dutch to find a water route west from Europe to China. He first sailed up the Hudson River in 1609.

The place still continues under the sway of some witching power that holds a spell over the minds of the people. They are given to all kinds of marvelous beliefs, are subject to trances and visions, and frequently see strange sights and hear music and voices. The place abounds with local tales, haunted spots, twilight superstitions and nightmares.

The dominant spirit that haunts this enchanted region is a headless figure on horseback. It is said by some to be the ghost of a **Hessian** trooper whose head had been carried away by a cannonball in a battle during the Revolutionary

THE SPIRIT THAT HAUNTS THIS REGION
IS A HEADLESS FIGURE ON HORSEBACK.

War, and who has been seen ever since by the country folk hurrying along in the gloom of night as if on the wings of the wind.

His haunts are not confined to the valley, but extend at times to the adjacent roads, and especially to the vicinity of a local church. Indeed, some local historians claim that the body of the trooper was buried in the churchyard and the ghost rides to the scene of battle every night in quest of his head. The rushing speed with which he sometimes passes along the hollow, like a midnight blast, is owing to his being late and in a hurry to get back to the churchyard before daybreak.

HESSIAN
A German soldier hired by the British during the American Revolution to fight against the colonists.

This legendary superstition has furnished materials for many a wild story in that region of shadows, and the specter is known, by all the country firesides, by the name of The Headless Horseman of Sleepy Hollow.

Everyone who resides there for a time is sure to inhale the witching influence of the air and begin to dream and see spirits.

In this place there lived a worthy fellow from Connecticut by the name of Ichabod Crane, who settled, or "tarried" as he expressed it, in Sleepy Hollow for the purpose of instructing the children of the vicinity. The name of Crane was well suited to him. He was tall and very lank, with narrow shoulders, long arms and legs, hands that dangled a mile out of his sleeves, and feet that might have served for shovels. His whole frame hung together most loosely. His head was small, and flat at the top, with huge ears, large green eyes, and a nose so long that it looked like a weathercock perched on his head to tell which way the wind blew. To see him striding along on a windy day with his clothes fluttering about him, one might have mistaken him for a scarecrow escaped from a cornfield.

His schoolhouse was a low building of one large room, rudely constructed of logs. The windows were partly patched with pages of old copy books. The schoolhouse stood in a rather lonely but pleasant spot, just at the foot of a woody hill, with a brook running close by and a large birch tree growing at one end of it. From there the low murmur of his pupils'

ONE MIGHT HAVE MISTAKEN HIM FOR A SCARECROW
ESCAPED FROM A CORNFIELD.

BIRCH
A rod made from a birch branch used to strike someone as punishment.

voices reciting their lessons might be heard on a drowsy summer's day, like the hum of a beehive, interrupted now and then by the authoritative voice of the master, or by the appalling sound of the **birch**, as he urged one of his students along the path of knowledge. He was a conscientious man who believed in the principle of "**spare the rod and spoil the child.**" Ichabod Crane's scholars certainly were not spoiled.

He administered justice with good judgement rather than severity, taking the burden off the backs of the weak and laying it on those of the strong. A puny lad who winced at the least flourish of the rod was passed by with indulgence, but justice was satisfied by inflicting a double portion on some tough, wrongheaded urchin who grew stubborn and sullen beneath the birch. All

SPARE THE ROD AND SPOIL THE CHILD
A saying from the Bible (Book of Proverbs, 13:24) meaning that children need physical punishment in order to develop properly.

this he called "doing his duty by their parents," and he followed it by the assurance that the smarting urchin "would remember it and thank him for it the longest day he had to live."

When school hours were over, he was the companion and playmate of the larger boys. On holiday afternoons he would walk some of the smaller ones home, who happened to have pretty sisters or good housewives for mothers, noted for their cooking. Indeed, it behooved him to keep on good terms with his pupils. The income from his school was small, and would have been scarcely sufficient to furnish him with daily bread, for he was a huge feeder. According to country custom, he stayed at the houses of the farmers whose children he instructed. With these he lived a week at a time, thus going the rounds of the neighborhood, with all his worldly effects tied up in a cotton handkerchief.

So all this might not be too much for the purses of rustic patrons, who are apt to consider the costs of schooling a severe burden and schoolmasters as lazy, he made himself both useful and agreeable. He assisted the farmers occasionally in the lighter labors of their farms. He helped make hay, mended the fences, took the horses to water, drove the cows from pasture, and cut wood. He helped mothers by sitting with a child on one knee and rocking a cradle with his foot for hours.

In addition to his other work, he was the singing master, and picked up many bright shillings by instructing the young folks in singing psalms. It was a matter of no little vanity to him on Sundays to take his station in front of the church with a band of chosen singers. His voice sounded far above all the rest of the congregation, and there are peculiar sounds still

PECULIAR SOUNDS STILL TO BE HEARD IN THAT CHURCH ARE
DESCENDED FROM THE NOSE OF ICHABOD CRANE.

to be heard in that church which are said to be descended from the nose of Ichabod Crane. Thus, **"by hook or crook"** the worthy scholar got along well enough, and was thought, by those who understood nothing of the demands of teaching, to have a wonderfully easy life of it.

The schoolmaster is generally a man of some importance in the female circle of a rural neighborhood, being considered a gentleman of vastly superior taste and accomplishments to rough country men, and, indeed, inferior in learning only to the parson. His appearance, therefore, is likely to cause a little stir at the tea table of a farmhouse, and the addition of a special dish of cakes or candies, or the parade of a silver teapot.

Ichabod was happy in the smiles of all the country damsels. He moved among them in the churchyard, between services on Sundays—gathering grapes for them from the wild vines that overran the surrounding trees, reciting for their amusement all the epitaphs on the tombstones, or sauntering, with a group of them, along the banks of the

BY HOOK OR CROOK
By any way possible, whether fair or not.

WHAT FEARFUL SHAPES AND SHADOWS LAY IN HIS PATH.

adjacent mill pond, while more bashful fellows hung sheep-
ishly back, envying his superior elegance and
way of talking.

In his wandering life he carried local
gossip from house to house, so that his
appearance was always greeted with satisfaction. He was also admired by the women as
a man of great learning, for he had read
several books all the way through, and
was a perfect master of **Cotton Mather**'s
History of New England Witchcraft, in
which, by the way, he most firmly believed.

COTTON MATHER was an influential American Puritan clergyman and author who played a leading part in the witch trials in Salem, Massachusetts, in 1692.

His appetite for ghosts and spirits was extraordinary,
and had been increased by his residence in this spellbound
region. No tale was too monstrous for him. It was often his
delight, after school was dismissed, to stretch himself on the
rich bed of clover bordering the little brook by the schoolhouse and there read dreadful tales until the gathering dusk of
evening made the printed page a mist before his eyes. Then, as
he wended his way by swamp and stream and woodland to the
farmhouse where he happened to stay, every
sound fluttered his excited imagination: the
moan of the **whippoorwill**; the cry of the tree
toad; the dreary hooting of the screech owl or

WHIPPOORWILL A bird heard only at night that is named for the sound it makes.

KATRINA VAN TASSEL WAS A BLOOMING LASS OF EIGHTEEN.

the sudden rustling of birds in a thicket, frightened from their roost. The fireflies, too, which sparkled most vividly in the darkest places, now and then startled him. If, by chance, a huge beetle came blundering in flight against him, he was ready to give up the ghost, with the idea that he was struck with a witch's token. His only resource on such occasions, either to drown thought, or drive away evil spirits, was to sing psalm tunes. The good people of Sleepy Hollow, as they sat by their doors in the evening, were often filled with awe at hearing his nasal melody floating from the distant hill or along the dusky road.

Another of his sources of fearful pleasure was to pass long winter evenings with the old Dutch wives as they sat spinning by the fire with a row of apples roasting along the hearth, and listening to their marvelous tales of ghosts and goblins and particularly of the headless horseman. Ichabod would delight them with his stories of witchcraft, and would frighten them with speculations about comets and shooting stars, and with the alarming fact that the world turns round and that half the time they were topsy-turvy!

But if there was a pleasure in all this, while cuddling in the glow of a crackling wood fire, and where, of course, no specter dared to show its face, it was dearly paid for by the terrors of his walk home. What fearful shapes and shadows lay in his path, amidst the dim and ghastly glare of a snowy night!

How often he was frightened by some shrub covered with snow, like a sheeted specter in his very path! How often did he shrink at the sound of his own steps, and dread to look over his shoulder, lest he should behold something tramping close behind him!

All these, however, were mere terrors of the night, and though he had seen many specters in his time, and more than once in his lonely walks had been set upon by Satan in different shapes, daylight put an end to all these evils. He would have passed a pleasant life of it, despite the Devil and all his works, if his path had not been crossed by a being that perplexes mortal man more than ghosts, goblins, and the whole race of witches put together, and that was—woman.

Among those who assembled each week to receive his instructions in singing was Katrina Van Tassel, the daughter and only child of a prosperous Dutch farmer. She was a blooming lass of eighteen, plump as a partridge, rosy-cheeked as one of her father's peaches, and universally known, not merely for her beauty, but her vast inheritance. She was a flirt, as might be perceived even in her dress, which was a mixture of ancient and modern fashions well suited to set off her charms. She wore jewelry of pure gold, which her great-great- grandmother had brought over from Holland,

and a short petticoat to display the prettiest foot and ankle in the country round.

Ichabod Crane had a soft and foolish heart toward women, and it is not to be wondered at 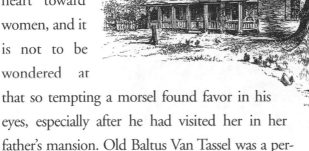 that so tempting a morsel found favor in his eyes, especially after he had visited her in her father's mansion. Old Baltus Van Tassel was a perfect picture of a thriving, contented farmer. He seldom sent either his eyes or his thoughts beyond the boundaries of his own farm, but within those everything was snug, happy, and well conditioned. He was satisfied with his wealth, but not proud of it, and prided himself upon the hearty abundance, rather than the style in which he lived. His stronghold was situated on the banks of the Hudson in one of those green, fertile nooks in which Dutch farmers often nestled. A great elm tree spread its broad branches over it, at the foot of which bubbled up a spring of the softest and sweetest water. By the farmhouse was a vast barn that might have served for a church. Every window and crevice seemed bursting forth with the treasures of the

HE PICTURED TO HIMSELF EVERY ROASTING PIG
WITH AN APPLE IN ITS MOUTH.

farm. Swallows and martins skimmed twittering about the eaves, and rows of pigeons enjoyed the sunshine on the roof. A stately squadron of snowy geese rode in an adjoining pond, regiments of turkeys gobbled through the farmyard, and guinea fowls fretted about with peevish cries. Before the barn door strutted the gallant cock, flapping his burnished wings and crowing in pride and gladness.

The schoolmaster's mouth watered as he looked upon this promise of luxurious winter fare. He pictured to himself every roasting pig running about with an apple in his mouth; the pigeons snugly put to bed in a pie and tucked in with a coverlet of crust; the geese swimming in their own gravy, and the ducks paired cozily in dishes, like snug married couples, with a decent amount of onion sauce; each turkey he imagined daintily tied up, with a necklace of savory sausages.

As Ichabod fancied all this, and as he rolled his great green eyes over the fat meadowlands, the rich fields of wheat, rye buckwheat, and Indian corn, and the surrounding orchards full of ruddy fruit, his heart yearned after the damsel who was to inherit these fields, and he imagined how they might be readily turned into cash and the money invested in vast tracts of land and palaces in the wilderness. His busy imagination already presented to him the blooming Katrina with a whole family of children, mounted on the top of a wagon loaded with household goods, with pots and kettles dangling beneath, and he pictured himself on a pacing mare, with a colt at her heels, setting out for Kentucky, Tennessee, or the Lord knows where!

When he entered the house, the conquest of his heart was complete. It was one of those spacious farmhouses, with high ridged but lowly sloping roofs, built in the style handed down from the first Dutch settlers. The low, projecting eaves formed a porch along the front, which could be closed up in bad weather. From this porch Ichabod entered the hall, where rows of shining **pewter**, ranged on a long dresser, dazzled his eyes. In one corner stood a huge bag of wool ready to be spun; in another a quantity of **linsey-woolsey** just from the loom; ears of Indian corn and strings of dried apples and peaches hung along the walls. A door left ajar gave him a peep into the best parlor, where the clawfooted chairs and dark mahogany tables shone like mirrors. Mock oranges and conch shells decorated the mantlepiece, strings of various colored birds' eggs

PEWTER
A silver-colored alloy made by combining tin with other metals. In colonial times, it was used to make plates, cups, bowls, platters and utensils.

LINSEY-WOOLSEY
A sturdy fabric of wool and linen or cotton.

were suspended above it, and a corner cupboard displayed immense treasures of old silver and china.

From the moment Ichabod laid his eyes upon these things his peace of mind was at an end. His only thought was how to gain the affections of the daughter of Van Tassel. In this enterprise, however, he had more real difficulties than generally fell to a knight of old, who seldom had anything but giants, sorcerers, fiery dragons, and other easily conquered adversaries to contend with. Ichabod had to win his way to the heart of a country coquette, with her maze of whims, which were forever presenting new difficulties; and he had to face a host of rustic admirers who kept a watchful and angry eye upon each other, ready to fly in common cause against any new competitor.

Among these the most formidable was a burly, dashing fellow named Brom Van Brunt, a local hero known for his feats of strength. He was broad shouldered, with short curly black hair, a large, but not unpleasant countenance, and an air of fun and arrogance. From his size and great strength he had received the nickname of Brom Bones. He was famed for great skill in horsemanship, was foremost at all races and cockfights, and was the umpire of all disputes. He was always ready for either a fight or a frolic, but had more mischief than ill-will in him. With all his roughness, there was a strong dash of good humor underneath. He had three or four companions who regarded him as their model, and with them he scoured the country, attending every scene of feud or merriment for miles round. Sometimes his crew would be heard dashing along past the farmhouses at midnight with whoops like a troop of **Cossacks**, and the old dames, startled out of their sleep, would listen for a moment till the hurry-scurry had clattered by, and then exclaim, "Aye, there goes Brom Bones and his gang!" The neighbors looked upon him with a mixture of awe, admiration, and good will, and when any madcap prank or rustic brawl occurred in the vicinity, they shook their heads and bet Brom Bones was at the bottom of it.

COSSACKS
People of southern Russia who gained fame as daring cavalrymen.

This hero had for some time singled out the blooming Katrina for the object of his gallantries, and it was whispered that she did not altogether discourage his hopes. His advances were signals for rival candidates to retire; they felt no inclination to cross a lion in his affections. When Brom's horse was seen tied to Van Tassel's fence on a Sunday night, all other suitors passed by in despair.

Such was the rival with whom Ichabod Crane had to contend. A stouter man than he would have shrunk from the competition, and a wiser man would have despaired. He had, however, a happy mixture of flexibility and perseverance in his nature. He was in form and spirit a supple fellow—yielding, but tough. Though he bent, he never broke, and though he bowed beneath the slightest pressure, the moment it was away he was erect again and carried his head as high as ever.

To have taken the field openly against his rival would have been madness. Ichabod, therefore, made his advances in a quiet manner. As singing master, he made frequent visits at the farmhouse. He had nothing to fear from the interference of parents, which is so often a stumbling block in the path of lovers. Balt Van Tassel was an easy, indulgent soul. He loved his daughter better even than his pipe, and like a reasonable man, and an excellent father, let her have her way in everything. His wife, too, had enough to do to attend to her housekeeping and manage her poultry, for, as she wisely observed, ducks and geese are foolish things, and must be looked after, but girls can take care of themselves. Thus while the busy dame bustled about the house, or worked at her spinning wheel at one end of the porch, honest Balt would sit smoking his evening pipe at the other. In the meantime, Ichabod would carry on his courtship with the daughter under the great elm, or sauntering along in the twilight, that hour so favorable to the lover's eloquence.

It is a mystery to me how women's hearts are wooed and won. Some seem to have but one vulnerable point, while others may be captured in a thousand different ways. It is a great triumph to gain the former, but a still greater triumph to keep possession of the latter. He who wins a thousand common hearts is therefore entitled to some renown, but he who keeps sway over the heart of a coquette is indeed a hero. Indeed, this was not the case with Brom Bones. From the moment Ichabod Crane made his advances, the interests of Brom Bones declined; his horse was no longer seen tied at the fence palings on Sunday nights, and a deadly feud gradually arose between him and the schoolmaster of Sleepy Hollow.

Brom, who had a degree of chivalry in his nature, would have carried matters to open warfare, but Ichabod had overheard a boast of Bones that he would "double the schoolmaster up and lay him on a shelf," and he was too wary to give him an opportunity. This left Brom no alternative but to play crude practical jokes upon his rival. Ichabod became the object of whimsical persecution to Bones and his gang of rough riders. They smoked out his singing school by stopping up the chimney. They broke into the schoolhouse at night and turned everything topsy-turvy, so that the poor schoolmaster began to think all the witches in the country held their meetings there. But what was still more annoying, Brom took all opportunities of ridiculing him in the presence of the blooming Katrina.

One fine autumn afternoon, Ichabod, in a pensive mood, sat on the lofty stool from where he watched over his realm. The birch rod was on three nails behind the stool, a constant terror to evil doers. On the desk before him were prohibited articles he had found in possession of idle urchins, such as half-munched apples, popguns, whirligigs and fly cages. Apparently there had been some act of justice recently inflicted, for his scholars were all busily intent upon their books, or slyly whispering behind them with one eye kept upon the master. A kind of buzzing stillness reigned throughout the schoolroom. It was suddenly interrupted by a man mounted on a wild colt who came to the door with an invitation for Ichabod to attend a merry making that evening at **Mynheer** Van Tassel's.

MYNHEER Dutch for "Mister".

The school was turned loose an hour before the usual time, and the children burst forth yelping in joy at their early release.

The gallant Ichabod spent at least a half hour brushing his suit of rusty black and arranging his locks by a bit of broken looking-glass that hung in the schoolhouse. He borrowed a horse from the farmer with whom he was staying, a

Dutchman of the name of Hans Van Ripper, and thus mounted, issued forth like a knight in quest of adventures. In the true
spirit of romantic story there should be some account of the
hero and his steed. The animal he rode was a broken-down
plow horse. He was gaunt and shaggy, with a thin neck and a
head like a hammer. His rusty mane and tail were tangled and
knotted with burrs. One eye had lost its pupil and was glaring
and spectral, but the other had the gleam of a genuine devil in
it. He must have had fire in him in his day, judging by the
name he bore: Gunpowder.

Ichabod was a suitable figure for such a steed. He rode
with short stirrups, which brought his knees nearly up to the

Pommel

POMMEL
**The mound
or knob on the
front of a
saddle.**

pommel of the saddle, and his sharp
elbows stuck out like grasshoppers'.
He carried his whip in his hand like
a scepter, and as his horse jogged
on, his arms flapped like a pair of
wings. A small wool hat rested on
the top of Ichabod's nose, and the
skirts of his black coat fluttered out
almost to the horse's tail.

It was, as I said, a fine autumn day. The sky was clear
and serene. The forests had put on their sober brown and yellow, and some trees had been nipped by frost into brilliant

orange, purple, and scarlet. Files of wild ducks made their appearance high in the air. As Ichabod jogged slowly on his way, his eye was open to every sign of abundance. He saw vast stores of apples, some hanging heavily on the trees, some gathered into baskets and barrels for the market, others heaped up in piles for the cider press. Further on there were great fields of Indian corn, holding out the promise of cakes and cornmeal pudding, and yellow pumpkins lying beneath the golden ears, turning up their round bellies to the sun and giving prospects of luxurious pies. As he passed the fragrant buckwheat fields, he breathed the odor of the beehive, and he thought of dainty slapjacks, well buttered and garnished with honey or syrup by the delicate dimpled hand of Katrina Van Tassel.

Thus feeding his mind with many sweet thoughts, he journeyed along a range of hills overlooking the mighty Hudson. The wide Tappan Zee lay motionless and glassy. Here and there a gentle wave prolonged the blue shadows of the distant mountain.

Toward evening Ichabod arrived at the castle of Heer Van Tassel, crowded with leather-faced farmers in homespun coats and breeches, blue stockings, and huge shoes with magnificent pewter buckles. Their little wives wore close-crimped caps, longwaisted gowns, and homespun petticoats with scissors and pincushions and gay calico pockets hanging on the outside. Brom Bones, however, was the hero of the scene, having come to the gathering on his favorite steed, Daredevil, a creature, like himself, full of mischief, which no one else could manage.

As Ichabod entered the parlor of Van Tassel's mansion, his gaze fell on the ample charms of a Dutch country tea table. There were doughnuts, sweet cakes and short cakes, ginger cakes and honey cakes. And there were apple pies and peach pies and pumpkin pies; slices of ham and smoked beef; and delectable dishes of preserved plums, and peaches, and pears; not to mention broiled shad and roasted chickens, and bowls of milk and cream, with the teapot sending up its clouds of vapor from the center of it all. Ichabod Crane did justice to every dainty.

He was a kind and thankful creature, whose spirits rose with eating as some men's do with drink. He could not help, too, rolling his large eyes round him as he ate, and chuckling with the possibility that he might one day be lord of this luxury. Then, he thought, how soon he'd turn his back upon the old schoolhouse, snap his fingers in the face of Hans Van Ripper and every other stingy patron, and kick any schoolteacher out of doors that should dare to call him comrade!

Old Baltus Van Tassel moved about among his guests with a face full with good humor, round and jolly as the har-

NOT A LIMB, NOT A FIBER ABOUT HIM WAS IDLE.

vest moon. His hospitable attentions were brief, being confined to a shake of the hand, a slap on the shoulder, a loud laugh, and a pressing invitation to "fall to, and help themselves."

And now the sound of the music from the hall summoned everyone to the dance. The musician scraped away on two or three strings of his fiddle, accompanying every movement of the bow with a motion of the head, bowing almost to the ground and stamping with his foot whenever a fresh couple started.

Ichabod prided himself upon his dancing as much as upon his vocal powers. Not a limb, not a fiber about him was idle, and to have seen his loosely hung frame in full motion and clattering about the room, you would have thought Saint Vitus himself, that blessed patron of dance, was moving before you in person. How could Ichabod be otherwise than joyous? The lady of his heart was his partner in the dance and smiling graciously in reply to all his amorous oglings, while Brom Bones, sorely smitten with love and jealousy, sat brooding by himself in one corner.

THE WAR
The American Revolution, 1776-1782

When the dance was at an end, Ichabod was attracted to a group of folks, who, with old Van Tassel, sat smoking at one end of the porch, gossiping over former times and telling long stories about **the war.**

This neighborhood was one of those highly favored places which abound with chronicle and great men. The British and American line had run near it during the war. It had, therefore, been the scene of raiding and just sufficient time had elapsed to enable each storyteller to dress up his tale with a little fiction and make himself the hero of every exploit.

But these were nothing compared to the tales of ghosts that followed. Local tales and superstitions thrive best in these sheltered, long settled retreats. In most villages, the ghosts have scarce had time to finish their first nap and turn themselves in their graves before their surviving friends have travelled away from the neighborhood, so that when the ghosts walk the rounds at night, they have no friends left to call upon.

The immediate cause of the supernatural stories in these parts was doubtless owing to the vicinity of Sleepy Hollow. There was in the very air that blew from that haunted region an atmosphere of dreams and fancies that infected all the land. Several of the Sleepy Hollow people were present at Van Tassel's, and, as usual, were doling out their wild legends. Many dismal tales were told about the wailings heard about the tree where **Major André** was taken. Mention was made of the woman in white that haunted the dark glen at Raven Rock. She perished there in the

JOHN ANDRÉ
A dashing British spy, linked with the American traitor Benedict Arnold, who was captured and hung by George Washington near Tarrytown, New York, in 1780.

snow, and was often heard to shriek on winter nights before a storm. But most of the stories turned upon the favorite specter of Sleepy Hollow, the headless horseman, who had been heard several times of late, patroling the country. It was said he tethered his horse nightly among the graves near the church.

This church seems to have been a favorite haunt of troubled spirits. It stands on a knoll, surrounded by locust trees and lofty elms, from among which its whitewashed walls shine forth like Christian purity. On one side of the church extends a wide woody dell, along which raves a large brook among broken rocks and trunks of fallen trees. Over a deep, black part of the stream, not far from the church, lay a wooden bridge. The road that led to it, and the bridge itself, were thickly shaded by overhanging trees, which cast a gloom even in the daytime and caused a fearful darkness at night.

Such was one of the favorite haunts of the headless horseman, and the place where he was most frequently encountered. The tale was told of how old Brouwer, a disbeliever in ghosts, met the horseman returning from Sleepy Hollow, was forced to get up behind him, and how they galloped over hill and swamp until they reached the bridge, when the horseman suddenly turned into a skeleton, threw old Brouwer into the brook, and sprang away over the treetops with a clap of thunder.

This story was immediately matched by Brom Bones, who said that on returning one night from a neighboring village, he had been overtaken by this midnight trooper. He had offered to race with him for a bowl of punch, and should have won too, for Daredevil beat the goblin horse, but just as they came to the church bridge the Hessian vanished in a flash of fire.

All these tales, told in that drowsy undertone with which men talk in the dark, sank deep in the mind of Ichabod. He repaid them in kind with stories of his own from Cotton Mather and fearful sights which he had seen in his nightly walks about Sleepy Hollow.

The party gradually broke up. The old farmers gathered their families in their wagons and were heard for some time rattling along the hollow roads and over the distant hills. Lighthearted laughter, mingling with the clatter of hoofs, echoed along the silent woodlands, sounding fainter and fainter until they gradually died away. Ichabod lingered behind, according to the custom of country lovers, to have a **tête-à-tête** with Katrina, fully convinced that he was now on the high road to success. Something, however, must have gone wrong, for he soon came out, quite desolate.

TÊTE-À-TÊTE
A French expression meaning to have a private conversation; literally, to be head to head.

Was the girl's encouragement of him a mere sham to win her conquest of his rival? Heaven only knows! Without looking to the right or left to notice the scene of rural wealth on which he had so often gloated, he went straight to the stable and roused his steed.

It was the very witching time of night that Ichabod, heavy hearted, traveled homewards, along the sides of the lofty hills which rise above Tarry Town, which he had passed so cheerily in the afternoon. The hour was as dismal as he was. Far below him the Tappan Zee spread its waters, with here and there the tall mast of a sailing ship riding quietly at anchor. In the dead hush of midnight, he could even hear the barking of the watch dog from the opposite shore of the Hudson. Now and then, too, the long-drawn crowing of a cock, accidentally awakened, would sound far, far off from some farmhouse among the hills.

All the stories of ghosts and goblins that he had heard in the afternoon now came crowding upon his recollection. The night grew darker and darker. The stars seemed to sink deeper in the sky, and driving clouds occasionally hid them from his sight. He had never felt so lonely and dismal. He was, moreover, approaching the very scene of many ghost stories. In the center of the road stood an enormous tulip tree, which towered like a giant above all the other trees of the neighborhood. Its limbs were gnarled and fantastic, large enough to form trunks for ordinary trees, twisting down almost to the earth and rising again into the air. The tree was connected to the tragic story of Major André, who had been taken prisoner nearby. It was now known as Major André's tree, and people regarded it with superstition.

As Ichabod approached this fearful tree, he began to whistle. He thought his whistle was answered, but it was only a blast sweeping sharply through the dry branches. As he approached a little nearer, he thought he saw something white hanging in the midst of the tree. He paused and ceased whistling, but on looking more closely, he perceived that it was a place where the tree had been scathed by lightning, and the white wood laid bare. Suddenly he heard a groan—his teeth chattered, and his knees hit against the saddle; it was but the rubbing of one huge bough upon another as they swayed about in the breeze. He passed the tree in safety, but new perils lay before him.

About two hundred yards from the tree, a small brook crossed the road and ran into a marsh and thickly wooded glen known as Wiley's Swamp. A few rough logs, laid side by side, served for a bridge over this stream. On that side of the road where the brook entered the wood, a group of oaks and chest-

INSTEAD OF STARTING FORWARD,
THE ANIMAL RAN BROADSIDE AGAINST A FENCE.

nuts, matted thick with wild grape vines, threw a cavernous gloom over it. To pass this bridge was the severest trial.

As he approached the stream, his heart began to thump. He summoned up all his courage, gave his horse half a score of kicks, and attempted to dash across the bridge. But instead of starting forward, the animal ran broadside against the fence. Ichabod, whose fears increased with the delay, jerked the reins on the other side and kicked with the opposite foot. It was all in vain. His steed started, but only to plunge to the opposite side of the road into a thicket of brambles and bushes. The schoolmaster now used both whip and heel on old Gunpowder, who dashed forward, snuffling and snorting, but came to a stand just by the bridge with a suddenness that nearly sent his rider sprawling over his head. Just at this moment a splash by the side of the bridge caught Ichabod's ear. In the dark shadow of the grove, on the margin of the brook, he saw something huge, misshapen, black and towering. It seemed gathered up in the gloom, like some gigantic monster ready to spring upon the traveller.

Ichabod's hair rose upon his head with terror. What was to be done? It was too late to turn and fly. And besides, what chance was there of escaping a ghost or goblin, if such it was, which could ride upon the wings of the wind? Summoning up a show of courage, he demanded in a stam-

A SCORE Twenty.

ICHABOD'S GARMENTS FLUTTERED
AS HE STRETCHED HIS LANK BODY OVER HIS HORSE'S HEAD.

mer, "Who are you?" He received no reply. He repeated his demand in a more agitated voice. Still there was no answer. Once more he beat the sides of Gunpowder, and shutting his eyes, began singing a psalm with fervor. Just then the shadowy object put itself in motion, and with a scramble and a bound, stood at once in the middle of the road. Though the night was dark, the form of the unknown might now be made out. He appeared to be a horseman of large dimensions mounted on a powerful black horse. He kept on one side of the road, jogging along on the blind side of old Gunpowder, who had now got over his fright.

Ichabod, who had no use for this midnight companion, now quickened his steed in hopes of leaving him behind. The stranger, however, quickened his horse to an equal pace. When Ichabod pulled up and fell into a walk, thinking to lag behind, the other did the same. Ichabod's heart began to sink within him. He tried to sing the psalm, but his parched tongue stuck to the roof of his mouth. There was something in the moody and dogged silence of this companion that was appalling. It was soon fearfully accounted for. On mounting a rising ground, which brought the figure of his fellow traveller in relief against the sky, Ichabod was horror struck on perceiving that he was headless! But his horror was increased on observing that the head, which should have rested on his shoulders, was carried before him on the pommel of the saddle! His terror rose to desperation. He rained a shower of kicks and blows upon Gunpowder, hoping to give his companion the slip—but the specter started full jump with him. Away they dashed, through thick and thin, stones flying and sparks flashing at every bound. Ichabod's garments fluttered in the air as he stretched his long lank body over his horse's head in eager flight.

They reached the road which turns off to Sleepy Hollow, but Gunpowder, who seemed possessed with a demon, instead of keeping on made an opposite turn and plunged headlong downhill to the left. This road leads through a sandy hollow shaded by trees for about a quarter of a mile, where it crosses the famous bridge, and just beyond swells the green knoll on which stands the whitewashed church.

As yet the panic of the steed had given his unskillful rider an advantage in the chase, but just as he had got half way through the hollow, the **girth** of the saddle gave way. Ichabod tried to hold it on, but in vain. He had just time to save himself by clasping old Gunpowder round the neck, when the saddle fell to the earth, and he heard it trampled under foot by his pursuer.

Girth

GIRTH
The strap that goes around the body of a horse to hold a saddle on.

For a moment the terror of Hans Van Ripper's anger passed across his mind, for it was his Sunday saddle. But this was no time for petty fears: the goblin was catching up, and he had to hang on. Slipping on one side, then the other, he was sometimes jolted on the high ridge of his horse's backbone with a violence that he feared would split him in two.

HE SAW THE GOBLIN IN THE VERY ACT OF HURLING HIS HEAD.

Ichabod saw the walls of the church dimly glaring under the trees beyond. He recollected the place where Brom Bones's ghostly competitor had disappeared. "If I can reach that bridge," thought Ichabod, "I am safe." Just then he heard the black steed panting and blowing close behind him. He even fancied that he felt his hot breath. Another kick in the ribs, and old Gunpowder sprung upon the bridge. He thundered over the planks, gained the opposite side, and now Ichabod cast a look behind to see if his pursuer would vanish, according to rule, in a flash of fire. Just then he saw the goblin rising in his stirrups in the very act of hurling his head at him. Ichabod tried to dodge the horrible missile, but too late. It encountered his cranium with a tremendous crash. He tumbled headlong into the dust, and Gunpowder, the black steed, and the goblin rider passed by like a whirlwind.

The next morning the old horse was found without his saddle, quietly cropping the grass at his master's gate. Ichabod did not make his appearance at breakfast. Dinner hour came, but no Ichabod. The boys assembled at the schoolhouse and strolled idly about the banks of the brook, but no schoolmaster. Hans Van Ripper now began to feel uneasy about the fate of poor Ichabod and his saddle. In a diligent search on foot, they came upon his traces. On the road leading to the church, they found the saddle trampled in the dirt. The tracks of horses' hoofs deeply dented the road, evidently at furious speed. They were traced to the bridge, beyond which, on the bank of a brook, was found the hat of the unfortunate Ichabod, and close beside it a shattered pumpkin.

The brook was searched, but the body of the schoolmaster was not discovered. Hans Van Ripper, as executor of his estate, examined the bundle which contained all his worldly goods. They consisted of two shirts, a pair or two of stockings, corduroy clothes, a rusty razor, a dog-eared book of psalm tunes, and a broken **pitch pipe**. As to the books and furniture of the schoolhouse, they belonged to the community, excepting Cotton Mather's *History of Witchcraft*, and a book of dreams and fortune telling in which was a sheet of paper much scribbled with several attempts to make verses in honor of the heiress of Van Tassel.

PITCH PIPE
A small, whistle-like pipe that is used to set the tone level when singing or tuning an instrument.

The books and poetic scrawl were thrown in the fire by Hans Van Ripper, who from that time forward determined to send his children no more to school, observing that he never knew any good to come of reading and writing. Whatever money the schoolmaster possessed, and he had received his quarter's pay but a day or two before, he must have had with him at the time of his disappearance.

The mysterious event caused much speculation at church on the following Sunday. Knots of gossips collected in the church yard, at the bridge, and at the spot where the hat and pumpkin had been found. The stories of Brouwer, of Bones, and others were called to mind. And when they had diligently considered them all, and compared them with the present case, they shook their heads and came to the conclusion that Ichabod had been carried off by the galloping Hessian. As he was a bachelor, and in nobody's debt, nobody troubled anymore about him. The school was moved to a different part of the hollow, and another scholar came to teach.

An old farmer who had been down to New York on a visit several years later brought home news that Ichabod Crane was still alive; that he had left the neighborhood partly through fear of the goblin and Hans Van Ripper, and partly in humiliation at having been suddenly dismissed by Katrina; that he had moved to a distant part of the country; had kept school and studied law at the same time; had been admitted to the bar, turned politician, written for newspapers, and finally had been made a Justice of the Court.

Shortly after his rival's disappearance, Brom Bones conducted the blooming Katrina in triumph to the altar. Whenever the story of Ichabod was told, he always burst into a hearty laugh at the mention of the pumpkin, which led some to suspect that he knew more about the matter than he chose to tell.

The old country wives, however, who are the best judges of these matters, maintain to this day that Ichabod was spirited away by supernatural means, and it is a favorite story often told round the evening fire. The bridge became more than ever an object of superstition, and that may be the reason why the road has since been altered to approach the church by the border of the millpond. The deserted schoolhouse soon fell to decay, and was reported to be haunted by the ghost of the unfortunate teacher. And the plowboy, walking home on a still summer evening, has often imagined Ichabod's voice at a distance, chanting a melancholy psalm tune in the peace and quiet of Sleepy Hollow.

HIS SENSES WERE OVERPOWERED AND HE FELL INTO A DEEP SLEEP

2

Rip Van Winkle

WHOEVER HAS MADE A VOYAGE UP THE HUDSON River must remember the Catskill mountains. They are a branch of the great Appalachians, and are seen away to the west swelling up to noble height and lording it over the surrounding country. Every change of season, every change of weather, indeed every hour of the day, produces some change in the magical hues and shapes of these mountains. When the weather is fair and settled, they are clothed in blue and purple and print their bold outlines on the clear evening sky. But sometimes, when the rest of the landscape is cloudless, they gather a hood of grey vapors about their summits, which, in the last rays of the setting sun, light up like a crown of glory.

At the foot of these fairy mountains the voyager may have seen smoke curling up from a village, whose shingle roofs gleam among the trees. The little village was founded by Dutch colonists at the time of **Peter Stuyvesant**. Some of the houses of the original settlers were still standing, built of small yellow bricks brought from Holland, with latticed windows and gable fronts and **weathercocks**.

PETER STUYVESANT
Administrator for the Dutch colonies in America in the mid-1600s.

Many years ago, when the country was still a province of Great Britain, a simple good natured fellow named Rip Van Winkle lived in one of these houses. He was a kind neighbor and an obedient, henpecked husband. He had a meekness of spirit which gained him wide pop-

WEATHERCOCKS
A turning metal piece often shaped like a rooster, mounted on the top of a building to indicate wind direction.

ularity, for the men most likely to be pleasing abroad are under the strict discipline of their wives at home. Their tempers are made flexible in the fiery furnace of domestic troubles, and a lecture from a wife in bed is worth all the sermons in the world for teaching the virtue of patience. A scolding wife may therefore in some respects be a blessing–if so, Rip Van Winkle was triple blessed.

HE ASSISTED THEIR SPORTS AND MADE THEIR PLAYTHINGS.

He was a great favorite among all the wives of the village, who took his part in all family squabbles and never failed, whenever they gossiped, to lay all the blame on Dame Van Winkle. The children of the village, too, would shout with joy whenever he approached. He assisted at their sports, made their playthings, taught them to fly kites and shoot marbles, and told them long stories of ghosts, witches and Indians. Whenever he went dodging about the village he was surrounded by a troop of them, clambering on his back and playing a thousand tricks on him. Not a dog would bark at him throughout the neighborhood.

The great error in Rip's composition was his strong dislike of profitable labor. He did not lack diligence or perseverance; he would sit on a wet rock holding a long and heavy rod and fish all day even without the encouragement of a single nibble. He trudged for hours through woods and swamps to shoot a few squirrels or wild pigeons. He would never refuse to assist a neighbor even in the roughest toil, and was there at all country frolics for husking Indian corn or building stone fences. The women of the village asked him to run their errands and to do odd jobs their less obliging husbands would not do for them. Rip was ready to attend to anybody's business but his own. As to keeping his farm in order, he found it impossible.

In fact, he declared it was of no use to work on his farm because it was the most unhealthy little piece of ground in the whole country. Everything about it went wrong in spite of him. His fences were continually falling to pieces; his cow would either go astray or get among the cabbages; weeds were sure to grow quicker in his fields than anywhere else; the rain always made a point of starting just as he had some outdoor work to do. His estate had dwindled away under his management until there was little more left than a mere patch of

Indian corn and potatoes. It was the worst farm in the neighborhood.

His children, too, were ragged and wild. His son Rip, an urchin created in his own likeness, promised to inherit the habits of his father. He was generally seen trooping like a colt at his mother's heels, dressed in a pair of his father's cast-off pants, which were so big he had to hold them up with one hand.

Rip Van Winkle, however, was one of those happy fools who take the world easy, eat white bread or brown, whichever can be got with least thought or trouble, and would rather starve on a penny than work for a pound. If left to himself, he would have whistled his life away in perfect contentment, but his wife continually complained in his ears about his idleness, his carelessness, and the ruin he was bringing on his family. Morning, noon and night her tongue was going. Rip had but one way of replying to all lectures of the kind. He shrugged his shoulders, shook his head, cast up his eyes, but said nothing. This always provoked a fresh volley from his wife, so that he left the house to go outside–the only side which belongs to a henpecked husband.

Rip's only ally at home was his dog Wolf, who was as much henpecked as his master, for Dame Van Winkle regarded them as companions in idleness. The moment Wolf entered

HIS WIFE CONTINUALLY COMPLAINED ABOUT HIS IDLENESS.

the house, his tail drooped to the ground or curled between his legs. He sneaked about, casting many a sidelong glance at Dame Van Winkle, and at the least wave of a broomstick or ladle he would fly to the door with a yelp.

Times grew worse and worse with Rip Van Winkle as years of matrimony rolled on. A tart temper never mellows with age, and a sharp tongue is the only edged tool that grows keener with constant use. He used to console himself when driven from home by frequenting a gathering of philosophers of the village which met on a bench before a small inn. Here they used to sit in the shade, through a long lazy summer's day, talking over village gossip, or telling endless sleepy stories about nothing. But it would have been worth any statesman's money to have heard the profound discussions that sometimes took place when by chance an old newspaper fell into their hands from some passing traveller. How solemnly they would listen to the contents as drawled out by Derrick Van Bummel the schoolmaster, a dapper, learned little man who was not daunted by the most gigantic word in the dictionary. And how sagely they would deliberate upon public events months after they had taken place.

The opinions of the group were completely controlled by Nicholaus Vedder, the landlord of the inn, at the door of which he took his seat from morning till night, moving just enough to avoid the sun and keep in the shade of a large tree, so that the neighbors could tell the hour by his movements as accurately as by a sundial. It is true he rarely spoke, but smoked his pipe constantly. His followers, however, perfectly understood him and knew how to gather his opinions. When anything displeased him, he smoked his pipe vehemently and sent forth short, frequent and angry puffs. When pleased, he inhaled the smoke slowly and tranquilly, releasing it in light

PROFOUND DISCUSSIONS TOOK PLACE
WHEN AN OLD NEWSPAPER FELL INTO THEIR HANDS.

and placid clouds, and sometimes, taking the pipe from his mouth and letting the fragrant vapor curl about his nose, he would gravely nod his head in approval.

From even this stronghold the unlucky Rip was driven by his scolding wife, who would suddenly break in and charge them with encouraging her husband in his idle habits.

Poor Rip was at last reduced almost to despair. His only alternative to escape from the labor of the farm and clamor of his wife was to take his gun and stroll into the woods.

Here he would sometimes sit at the foot of a tree and share his food with Wolf, with whom he sympathized as a fellow sufferer. Wolf would wag his tail and if dogs can feel pity, I believe he returned the sentiment with all his heart.

In a long ramble of this kind one fine autumn day, Rip had scrambled to one of the highest parts of the Catskill mountains for his favorite sport of squirrel shooting. The stillness echoed and re-echoed with the reports of his gun. Panting and fatigued, he threw himself, late in the afternoon, on a green knoll that crowned the brow of a cliff. From an opening between the trees he could overlook all the lower country for many miles. He saw at a distance the lordly Hudson, far below him, moving on its majestic course, with the reflection of a purple cloud, or the sail of a ship here and there, and at last losing itself in the blue highlands.

On the other side he looked down into a deep mountain glen, wild and lonely, scarcely lighted by the rays of the setting sun. For some time Rip lay musing on this scene. Evening gradually advanced, and the mountains began to throw their long blue shadows over the valleys. He saw that it would be dark long before he could reach the village, and he heaved a heavy sigh when he thought of encountering the terrors of Dame Van Winkle.

As he was about to descend he heard a voice from a distance hallooing "Rip Van Winkle! Rip Van Winkle!" Wolf bristled up his back, and giving a low growl, skulked to his master's side, looking fearfully down into the glen. Rip now felt a vague fear stealing over him. He looked anxiously in the same direction and saw a strange figure slowly toiling up the rocks and bending under the weight of something he carried on his back. He was surprised to see any human being in this lonely place, but supposing it to be someone in need of his assistance, he hurried down to give it.

As he came nearer, he was still more surprised at the stranger's unusual appearance. He was a short, square-built old fellow, with thick bushy hair and a grizzled beard. His dress was of antique Dutch fashion: a cloth **jerkin** strapped round the waist, and breeches decorated with rows of buttons down the sides. He bore on his shoulder a stout keg full of liquor, and made signs for Rip to assist him with the load. Though rather shy and distrustful of this new acquaintance, Rip complied, and they clambered up a narrow gully, apparently the dry bed of a mountain torrent. As they climbed, Rip every now and then heard long rolling peals like distant thunder that seemed to

JERKIN
A sleeveless, close-fitting jacket that covered the hips.

issue out of a deep ravine between lofty rocks, toward which their rugged path was headed. Supposing it to be the muttering of one of those passing thundershowers which often take place in mountain heights, Rip proceeded. Passing through the ravine they came to a hollow like a small amphitheater, surrounded by rock cliffs. During the whole time Rip and his companion labored on in silence.

On entering the amphitheater, new objects of wonder presented themselves. On a level spot in the center was a company of odd looking men playing **ninepins**. They were dressed in outlandish fashion—they wore close-fitting jackets, with long knives in their belts, and most of them had enormous britches. Their faces, too, were peculiar. One had a large head, broad face, and small piggish eyes. The face of another seemed to consist entirely of nose, and was topped by a large, white hat set off with a red feather. They all had beards of various shapes and colors. There was one who seemed to be the commander. He was a stout old gentleman, with a weatherbeaten face. He wore a laced **doublet**, broad belt, high crowned hat and feather, red stockings and high heeled shoes with roses in them. The group reminded

NINEPINS
A bowling game.

DOUBLET
A man's jacket similar to a jerkin, but made of two layers that were quilted.

Rip of the figures in an old painting in the parlor of the village parson, which had been brought over from Holland at the time of the settlement.

What seemed particularly odd to Rip was that though these folks were amusing themselves, they maintained the gravest faces, the most mysterious silence, and were, in fact, the most melancholy party he had ever witnessed. Nothing interrupted the stillness of the scene but the noise of the balls, which, whenever they were rolled, echoed along the mountains like rumbling thunder.

As Rip and his companion approached them they suddenly stopped playing and stared at him with such fixed statue-like gazes that his heart turned within him and his knees knocked together. His companion now emptied the contents of the keg into large **flagons** and made signs to him to wait upon the company. He obeyed with fear and trembling. They drank the liquor in silence and then returned to their game.

FLAGON
A large vessel with a handle, spout and lid, often used to hold wine.

By degrees Rip's awe subsided. He even ventured, when no eye was fixed upon him, to taste the beverage, which he found had the flavor of excellent Dutch gin. One taste invited another, and he repeated his visits to the flagon so often that at length his senses were overpowered and he fell into a deep sleep.

On awaking he found himself on the green knoll from where he had first seen the old man of the glen. He rubbed his eyes–it was a bright, sunny morning. The birds were hopping and twittering among the bushes, and the eagle was wheeling aloft in the pure mountain breeze. "Surely," thought Rip, "I have not slept here all night." He recalled what had happened before he fell asleep. The strange man with a keg of liquor–the mountain ravine–the wild retreat among the rocks–the woebegone party at ninepins–the flagon–"Oh! that wicked flagon!" thought Rip, "What excuse shall I make to Dame Van Winkle?"

He looked around for his gun, but in place of the clean, well oiled fowling piece he found an old one lying by him, the barrel encrusted with rust, the lock falling off and the stock worm-eaten. He now suspected that the men of the mountain had played a trick upon him, and having dosed him with liquor, had robbed him of his gun. Wolf, too, had disappeared, but he might have strayed away after a squirrel or partridge. He whistled after him and shouted his name–but all in vain; the echoes repeated his whistle and shout, but no dog was to be seen.

He determined to revisit the scene of the last evening's romp, and if he met with any of the party, to demand his dog and gun. As he arose to walk he found himself stiff in the joints. "These mountain beds do not agree with me," thought Rip, "and if this frolic should lay me up with a fit of the **rheumatism**, I shall have a blessed time with Dame Van Winkle." With some difficulty he got down into the glen. He found the gully up which he and his companion had climbed the preceding evening, but to his astonishment a mountain stream was now foaming down it, leaping from rock to rock, and filling the glen with babbling murmurs. He scrambled up its sides, working his way through thickets of birch, sassafras and witch hazel, sometimes tripped up by the wild grape vines that twisted their coils from tree to tree.

RHEUMATISM
Pain in the muscles and joints.

At length he reached where the ravine had opened to the amphitheater, but no traces of an opening remained. The rocks presented a high wall over which the torrent came tumbling in a sheet of feathery foam and fell into a broad deep basin black from the shadows of the surrounding forest. Here, then, poor Rip was brought to a stand. He again called and whistled after his dog–he was answered only by the cawing of a flock of idle crows, who seemed to look down and scoff at the poor man's perplexities.

What was to be done? The morning was passing away and Rip felt famished for his breakfast. He grieved to give up his dog and gun; he dreaded to meet his wife; but it would not do to starve in the mountains. He shook his head, shouldered the rusty gun, and with a heart full of trouble and anxiety, turned homeward.

As he approached the village he met a number of people, but none whom he knew, which somewhat surprised him, for he had thought himself acquainted with everyone in the country round. Their dress, too, was of a different fashion. They all stared at him with surprise and stroked their chins. This gesture caused Rip to do the same, and to his astonishment he found his beard had grown a foot long!

At the edge of the village, a troop of strange children ran at his heels, hooting after him and pointing at his grey beard. The dogs, too, not one of which he recognized, barked at him as he passed. The very village was altered it was larger and more populous. There were rows of houses he had never seen before, and his familiar haunts had disappeared. Strange names were over the doors, strange faces at the windows—everything was strange. He began to wonder whether both he and the world around him were not bewitched. Surely this was his native village which he had left but the day before. There stood the Catskill mountains—there ran the silver Hudson at a distance—there was every hill and dale precisely as it had always been. Rip was sorely perplexed. "That flagon last night," he thought, "has addled my poor head!"

RIP CALLED HIM BY NAME, BUT THE CUR SNARLED.

It was with some difficulty that he found the way to his own house, which he approached with silent awe, expecting every moment to hear the shrill voice of Dame Van Winkle. He found the house gone to decay–the roof fallen in, the windows shattered and the doors off the hinges. A half-starved dog that looked like Wolf was skulking about it. Rip called him by name, but the cur snarled and showed his teeth. "My very dog," sighed poor Rip, "has forgotten me!"

He entered the house, which Dame Van Winkle had always kept in neat order. It was empty, forlorn, and apparently abandoned. He called loudly for his wife and children–the lonely chambers rang for a moment with his voice, and then all again was silence.

He now hurried forth and hastened to the village inn–but it, too, was gone. A large, rickety wooden building stood in its place, with great gaping windows, some of them broken and mended with old hats and petticoats, and over the door was printed "The Union Hotel, by Jonathan Doolittle." Instead of the great tree that used to shelter the quiet little Dutch inn, there was now reared a tall pole and from it was fluttering a flag of stars and stripes. All this was strange. He recognized on the sign, however, the ruby face of **King George** under which he

KING GEORGE III
King of England during the time of the American Revolution.

had smoked many a peaceful pipe, but even this was different. The red coat was changed for one of blue and buff, a sword was held in the hand instead of a scepter; the head was decorated with a **cocked hat**, and underneath was printed in large characters GENERAL WASHINGTON.

There was as usual a crowd of folk about the door, but none that Rip recollected. The very character of the people seemed changed. There was a busy, bustling quarrelsome tone about it, instead of the usual drowsy tranquillity. He looked in vain for Nicholaus Vedder with his broad face, double chin and long pipe, uttering clouds of tobacco smoke instead of idle speeches. Or Van Bummel the schoolmaster doling forth the contents of an ancient newspaper.

In place of these, a lean, disagreeable-looking fellow with his pockets full of **handbills** was ranting about rights of citizens, elections, members of Congress, liberty, **Bunker Hill** and other things which made no sense to Rip Van Winkle.

The appearance of Rip with his long grizzled beard, his rusty gun, his outlandish dress and an army of women and

COCKED HAT
A hat with its brim turned up to make it three-cornered.

HANDBILLS
A small sheet of paper with an announcement printed on it, meant to be distributed by hand.

BUNKER HILL
In Boston, the site of an early battle in the American Revolution.

children at his heels soon attracted the attention of the tavern politicians. They crowded around him, eyeing him from head to foot with great curiosity. The orator bustled up to him and, drawing him aside, asked him how he voted. Rip stared in stupidity. Another fellow pulled him by the arm and asked in his ear whether he was Federal or Democrat. Rip was at a loss to understand the question, when an old gentlemen in a cocked hat made his way through the crowd, and planting himself before Van Winkle, his keen eyes and sharp hat seeming to look into Rip's very soul, demanded in an grave tone, "What brought him to the election with a gun on his shoulder and a mob at his heels, and whether he meant to start a riot in the village?"

"Alas, gentlemen," cried Rip, somewhat dismayed, "I am a poor quiet man, a native of the place, and a loyal subject of the King–God bless him!"

Here a general shout burst from the bystanders. "A **tory**! A tory! A spy! A refugee! Away with him!" It was with great difficulty that the self-important man in the cocked hat restored

TORY
The name for a colonist loyal to the British king during the American Revoultion.

order, and he demanded of Rip what he came there for and whom he was seeking. The poor man humbly assured him that he meant no harm, but merely came there in search of some of his neighbors, who used to meet at the tavern.

"Well–who are they? Name them."

Rip thought a moment and inquired, "Where's Nicholaus Vedder?"

There was silence for a little while. Then an old man replied, in a thin voice, "Nicholaus Vedder? Why he is dead and gone these eighteen years! There was a wooden tombstone in the church yard that used to tell all about him, but that's rotted and gone too."

"Where's Brom Dutcher?"

"Oh, he went off to the army in the beginning of the war. Some say he was killed at the storming of Stoney Point. Others say he was drowned in a squall. I don't know–he never came back again."

"Where's Van Bummel the schoolmaster?"

"He went off to the wars, too–was a great militia general and is now in Congress."

Rip's heart died away at hearing of these sad changes in his home and friends, and finding himself alone in the world. Every answer puzzled him, too, by including such enormous lapses of time and matters he could not understand–war, Congress, Stoney Point. He had no courage to ask after any more friends, but cried out in despair, "Does nobody here know Rip Van Winkle?"

"Oh. Rip Van Winkle?" exclaimed two or three. "Oh, to be sure! That's Rip Van Winkle yonder, leaning against the tree."

Rip beheld a precise copy of himself the day he went up the mountain, apparently as lazy and certainly as ragged! The poor fellow was now completely confounded. He doubted his own identity. In the midst of his bewilderment the man in the cocked hat demanded who he was and what was his name?

"God knows," he exclaimed, at his wit's end, "I'm not myself. That's me yonder–no–that's somebody else got into my shoes–I was myself last night, but I fell asleep on the mountain, and they've changed my gun, and everything's changed and I'm changed and I can't tell what's my name, or who I am!"

The bystanders began to look at each other, nod, wink, and tap their fingers against their foreheads. There was a whisper also about securing the gun and keeping the old fellow from doing mischief. At this critical moment a woman pressed through the throng to get a peep at the greybearded man. She had a chubby child in her arms, who began to cry. "Hush, Rip," cried she, "the old man won't hurt you." The name of the child and the tone of the mother's voice awakened a train of recollections in his mind. "What is your name, my good woman?" he asked.

"Judith Gardenier."

"And your father's name?"

"Rip Van Winkle was his name, but it's twenty years since he went away from home with his gun and never has been heard of since–his dog came home without him–but whether he shot himself, or was carried away by the Indians nobody can tell. I was then but a little girl."

Rip had but one question more to ask, but he put it with a faltering voice–

"Where's your mother?"

"She died but a short time ago. She broke a blood vessel in a fit of passion at a peddler."

There was a bit of comfort at least in this news. The honest man could contain himself no longer–he caught his daughter and her child in his arms. "I am your father!" he cried. "Young Rip Van Winkle once, old Rip Van Winkle now! Does nobody know Rip Van Winkle?"

All stood amazed, until an old woman tottering out from among the crowd put her hand to her brow, and peering under it in his face for a moment exclaimed, "Sure enough! It is Rip Van Winkle. Welcome home again, old neighbor. Where have you been these twenty long years?"

HENRY HUDSON'S SHIP, THE HALF MOON

Rip's story was soon told, for the whole twenty years had been to him but as one night. The neighbors stared when they heard it. Some winked at each other and put their tongues in their cheeks, and the self-important man in the cocked hat screwed down the corners of his mouth and shook his head—upon which there was a general shaking of the head throughout the crowd.

It was decided, however, to take the opinion of old Peter Vanderdonk, who was seen slowly advancing up the road. He was a descendant of the historian who wrote one of the earliest accounts of the province. Peter was the most ancient inhabitant of the village and well versed in all the wonderful events and traditions of the neighborhood. He recollected Rip at once, and confirmed his story. He assured the company that it was a fact handed down from his ancestor the historian that the Catskill mountains had always been haunted by strange beings. It was affirmed that the great Henry Hudson, the first discoverer of the river and country, kept a kind of vigil there every twenty years, with the crew of his ship, the Half Moon. In this way he could revisit the scenes of his enterprise and keep a guardian eye upon the river and the great city called by his name. Peter Vanderdonk's father had once seen them in their old Dutch clothes playing ninepins in a hollow of the mountain, and he himself had heard one summer afternoon the sound of their balls, like distant peals of thunder.

To make a long story short, the company broke up and returned to the more important concerns of the election. Rip's daughter took him home to live with her. She had a snug, well-furnished house, and a stout, cheery farmer for a husband whom Rip recollected as one of the urchins that used to climb upon his back. As for Rip's son and heir, who was a picture of

HE TOOK HIS PLACE ONCE MORE ON THE BENCH AT THE INN DOOR.

himself seen leaning against the tree, he was employed to work on the farm, but showed his father's tendency to attend to anything but his own business.

Rip now resumed his old walks and habits. He soon found many of his former cronies, though all rather the worse for the wear and tear of time, and preferred making friends among the rising generation, with whom he soon grew into great favor. Having nothing to do at home, and having arrived at that happy age when a man is allowed to be idle, he took his place once more on the bench at the inn door and was revered as one of the patriarchs of the village and a chronicle of the old times before the Revolutionary War.

It was some time before he could get into the regular track of gossip or could be made to comprehend the strange events that had taken place during his sleep. How there had been a revolutionary war—that the country had thrown off the yoke of Old England and that instead of being a subject of his majesty George the Third, he was now a free citizen of the United States. Rip in fact was no politician. The changes of states and empires made little impression on him. There was just one type of **despotism** under which he had long groaned, and that was petticoat government. Happily that was at an end. Now he could go in and out whenever he pleased without dreading the tyranny of Dame Van Winkle. Whenever her name was mentioned, however, he shook his head, shrugged his shoulders and cast up his eyes, which might pass either for an expression of resignation to his fate or joy at his deliverance.

DESPOTISM
A kind of government in which the ruler has unlimited power and may rule harshly.

He used to tell his story to every stranger who arrived at Mr. Doolittle's hotel. He was observed at first to vary on some points every time he told it, which was doubtless owing to his having so recently awakened. It at last settled down precisely to the tale I have related, and every man, woman and child in the neighborhood knew it by heart. Some always pretended to doubt the reality of it, and insisted that Rip had been out of his head. The old Dutch inhabitants, however, gave his story full credit. Even to this day they never hear a thunderstorm on a summer in the Catskills but they say Henry Hudson and his crew are at their game of ninepins; and it is a common wish of all henpecked husbands in the neighborhood, when life hangs heavy on their hands, that they might have a quieting drink from Rip Van Winkle's flagon.

THE AUNTS WERE STRICT SUPERVISORS
OF THE CONDUCT OF THEIR NIECE.

3

The Specter Bridegroom

ON A SUMMIT OVERLOOKING A WILD AND ROMANTIC part of Germany, near where the Rhine and Main rivers join, there stood many, many years ago the castle of the Baron Von Landshort. It is now fallen to decay, almost buried among beech trees and dark firs. Only the old watch tower still looks down upon the neighboring country.

The Baron had inherited the property, and all the pride of his ancestors. Though his family had lost many of its possessions in war, the Baron attempted to keep up some show of their former state. The times were peaceful, and most German nobles had abandoned their old castles, perched like eagles' nests among the mountains, and had built more convenient residences in the valleys. Still the Baron remained proudly drawn up in his little fortress, cherishing all the old family feuds, so that he was on ill terms with some of his nearest neighbors, on account of disputes that had happened between their great-great-grandfathers.

The Baron had but one child, a daughter, but nature, when she grants but one child, always makes up for that by making it a prodigy, and so it was with the daughter of the Baron. All the nurses, gossips, and country cousins assured her father that she had no equal for beauty in all Germany. She had, moreover, been brought up with great care by two maiden aunts, who were skilled in all the branches of knowledge necessary to the education of a fine lady. Under their instructions, she became a miracle of accomplishments. By the time she was eighteen she could embroider to admiration, and had worked whole histories of the saints in tapestry, with such strength of expression in their faces, that they looked like so many souls in **purgatory**. She could read, spell, and sign her own name so neatly that her aunts could read it without spectacles. She excelled in making little elegant knick-knacks of all kinds, was versed in the most difficult dancing of the day, played a number of tunes on the harp and guitar, and knew many tender ballads by heart.

PURGATORY
According to Roman Catholic belief, a place where people go after their deaths and suffer for the sins they committed until their souls are purified enough to go on to heaven.

Her aunts, having been great coquettes in their younger days, were now strict supervisors of the conduct of their niece. She was rarely let out of their sight, and never went beyond the grounds of the castle unless watched. She had lectures read to her about decorum and obedience, and she was taught to hold men at such distance and in such absolute distrust that, unless properly authorized, she would not have cast a glance upon the handsomest cavalier in the world—no, not even if he were dying at her feet!

The good effects of this system were wonderfully apparent. The young lady was a pattern of mildness and correctness. While others were wasting their sweetness in the glare of the world, perhaps only to be plucked and thrown aside, she was blooming into fresh and lovely womanhood under the protection of those flawless spinsters, like a rosebud blushing forth among guardian thorns. Her aunts looked upon her with pride, and believed that though all the other young ladies in the world might go astray, nothing of the kind could happen to the heiress of Katzenellenbogen.

But, however scantily the Baron Von Landshort might be provided with children, his household was by no means a small one, for he was blessed with an abundance of poor relations. They, one and all, possessed the affections common to humble relatives: they were wonderfully attached to the Baron, and took every possible occasion to come in swarms. All family festivals were hosted at the Baron's expense, and when they were filled with good cheer, these good people would declare that there was nothing on earth so delightful as these family meetings, these jubilees of the heart.

The Baron, though a small man, had a large soul, and it swelled with satisfaction at knowing he was the greatest man in the little world about him. He loved to tell long stories about the old warriors whose portraits looked grimly down from the walls around, and he found no listeners equal to those who fed at his expense. He was much given to the marvelous, and a firm believer in all those supernatural tales with which every mountain and valley in Germany abounds. The faith of his guests exceeded even his own. They listened to every tale of wonder with open eyes and mouth, and never failed to be astonished, even when they were repeated for the hundredth time.

At the time my story tells of, there was a great family gathering at the Castle to receive the bridegroom of the Baron's daughter. The girl's father and an old nobleman of Bavaria had agreed to unite their houses by the marriage of their children. The young people were betrothed without seeing each other, and the time was appointed for the marriage ceremony. The young Count Von Altenburg had been recalled from the army

THE BARON LOVED TO TELL LONG STORIES AND FOUND NO LISTENERS
EQUAL TO THOSE WHO FED AT HIS EXPENSE.

for the purpose and was on his way to the Baron's castle to receive his bride.

The castle was in a tumult of preparation to give him a suitable welcome. The fair bride had been decked out with uncommon care. The two aunts quarrelled the whole morning about every article of her dress. The young lady had taken advantage of their contest to follow her own taste, and fortunately it was a good one. She looked as lovely as a bridegroom could desire, and the flutter of expectation heightened the luster of her charms.

Her blush, the gentle heaving of her bosom, the eye now and then lost in reverie–all betrayed the excitement in her little heart. The aunts hovered around her, telling her how to behave, what to say, and how to receive her expected lover.

The Baron was no less busy. He had, in truth, nothing exactly to do, but he was naturally a bustling little man and could not remain still when all the world was in a hurry. He worried from the top to bottom of the castle; he continually called the servants from their work to tell them to be diligent and buzzed about every hall and chamber like a fly on a summer day.

In the meantime, the fatted calf had been killed; the forests had rung with the clamor of the huntsmen; the kitchen was crowded with good cheer; the cellars had yielded up oceans of wine. Everything was ready to receive the distinguished guest in the true spirit of German hospitality—but the guest delayed his appearance. Hour rolled after hour. The Baron mounted the highest tower and strained his eyes in hopes of catching sight of the Count and his attendants. Once he thought he beheld them; the sound of horns came floating from the valley, prolonged by the mountain echoes. A number of horsemen were seen far below, slowly advancing along the road, but when they had nearly reached the foot of the mountain, they suddenly struck off in a different direction. The last ray of sunshine departed—the bats began to flit by in the twilight—the road grew dimmer and dimmer, and nothing appeared to stir in it, but now and then a peasant lagging homeward from his labor.

While the old castle of Von Landshort was in this state of perplexity, a very interesting scene was taking place in a different part of the Oldenwald forest.

The young Count Von Altenburg was pursuing his route in that sober way in which a man travels towards matrimony when his friends have taken all the trouble and uncertainty of courtship off his hands. He had encountered at Wurtzburg a youthful companion with whom he had seen some service on the frontiers, Herman Von Starkenfaust, one of the stoutest hands, and worthiest hearts, of German chivalry,

THEY AGREED TO TRAVEL THE REST OF THEIR JOURNEY TOGETHER.

who was now returning from the army. His father's castle was not far distant from the old fortress of Von Landshort, although an ancient feud caused the families to be hostile, and strangers to each other.

In the warmhearted moment of recognition, the young friends related all their past adventures and fortunes, and the Count gave the whole history of his intended wedding with a young lady whom he had never seen, but of whose charms he had received the most wonderful descriptions.

As their route lay in the same direction, they agreed to travel the rest of their journey together. They set out at an early hour and the Count gave directions to his retinue to follow and overtake him.

Along the way they recollected their military adventures, but the Count was apt to be a little tedious, now and then, about the reputed charms of his bride and the happiness that awaited him.

In this way they entered one of its most lonely and thickly wooded passes in the mountains of Odenwald. It is well known that the forests of Germany have always been much infested by robbers, and, at this time, they were particularly numerous from the hordes of disbanded soldiers wandering about the country. The cavaliers were attacked by a gang of these stragglers in the midst of the forest. They defended

THEY DEFENDED THEMSELVES BRAVELY.

themselves bravely, but were nearly overpowered before the Count's men arrived to their assistance. At sight of them the robbers fled, but not until the Count had received a mortal wound. He was slowly and carefully conveyed back to the city of Wurtzburg, and a friar summoned from a neighboring convent who was famous for his skill in administering to both soul and body. But half of his skill was of no use. The moments of the unfortunate Count were numbered.

With his dying breath he asked his friend to go to the castle of Von Landshort and explain the fatal cause of his not keeping his appointment with his bride. He appeared concerned that this mission should be speedily executed. "Unless this is done," he said, "I shall not sleep quietly in my grave!" He repeated these last words with peculiar solemnity. A request at such a moment allowed no hesitation. Starkenfaust tried to calm him, promised faithfully to carry out his wish, and gave him his hand in solemn pledge. The dying man pressed it in acknowledgment, but soon lapsed into delirium and raved about his bride, his engagement, his promise. He ordered his horse that he might ride to the castle of Von Landshort, and died in the act of vaulting into the saddle.

Starkenfaust gave a sigh, and a soldier's tear, on the untimely fate of his comrade, and then pondered the mission he had undertaken. His heart was heavy and his head perplexed, for he was to present himself an uninvited guest among hostile people, and to dampen their festivity with tidings fatal to their hopes. Still he was curious to see this beauty of Katzenellenbogen, so shut up from the world, for he was a passionate admirer of women and fond of adventure.

Before his departure he made arrangements for the funeral of his friend, who was to be buried in the cathedral of Wurtzburg, near some of his illustrious relatives.

THE STRANGER AT THE GATE WAS A GALLANT CAVALIER
MOUNTED ON A BLACK STEED.

By this time, the ancient family of Katzenellenbogen was impatient for the guest, and still more for their dinner, and the Baron was waiting in the watch tower.

Night closed in, but still no guest arrived. The Baron descended from the tower in despair. The banquet, which had been delayed from hour to hour, could no longer be postponed. The meats were already overdone, the cook in agony, and the whole household had the look of a garrison that had been reduced to starvation. The Baron reluctantly gave orders for the feast to begin without the guest. All were seated at the table and just on the point of commencing, when the sound of a horn announced the approach of a stranger. Another long blast filled the old courts of the castle with its echoes and was answered by a guard. The Baron hastened to receive his future son-in-law.

The drawbridge had been let down, and the stranger was at the gate. He was a tall, gallant cavalier, mounted on a black steed. His face was pale, but he had a beaming, romantic eye, and a stately air. The Baron was a little shocked that he should have come in this simple, solitary style. His dignity for a moment was ruffled, and he considered it a lack of proper respect for the occasion, and the important family with which he was to be connected. He pacified himself with the conclusion that it must have been youthful impatience that made him spur on sooner than his attendants.

"I am sorry," said the stranger, "to break upon you so late–"

Here the Baron interrupted him with a world of compliments and greetings, for he prided himself on his courtesy and eloquence. The stranger tried once or twice to stem the torrent of words, but in vain, so he bowed his head and suffered it to flow on. By the time the Baron had come to a pause, they had reached the inner court of the castle and the stranger was again about to speak, when he was once more interrupted by the appearance of the female part of the family, leading the blushing bride. He gazed on her for a moment as one entranced. It seemed as if his whole soul beamed forth in the gaze and rested upon that lovely form. One of the maiden aunts whispered something in her ear and she made an effort to speak. She gave a shy glance on the stranger and cast her eyes again to the ground. The words died away, but there was a sweet smile playing about her lips and a soft dimpling of the cheek that showed her glance had not been unsatisfactory. It was impossible for a girl of eighteen ready for love and matrimony not to be pleased with so gallant a cavalier.

The late hour at which the guest had arrived left no time for further conversation. The Baron led the way to the untasted banquet.

It was served in the great hall of the castle. Around the walls hung portraits of the heroes of the house of Katzenellenbogen and the trophies which they had gained in the field and in the chase. Splintered spears and tattered banners mingled with the jaws of a wolf and the tusks of the boar, and a huge pair of antlers branched just over the head of the youthful bridegroom.

The cavalier took little notice of the company or the entertainment. He scarcely tasted the banquet, but seemed absorbed in admiration of his bride. He talked in a low tone that could not be overheard—for the language of love is never loud. There was a mingled tenderness and gravity in his manner that appeared to have a powerful effect upon the young lady. Her color came and went as she listened with deep attention. Now and then she made some blushing reply, and when his eye was turned away, she would steal a sidelong glance at him and heave a gentle sigh of happiness. The aunts, who were deeply knowledgeable of the mysteries of the heart, declared that the young couple had fallen in love with each other at first sight.

The feast went on merrily, or at least noisily, for the guests were all blessed with keen appetites. The Baron told his best and longest stories, and never had he told them so well. If there was anything marvelous, his listeners were lost in astonishment, and if anything was amusing, they were sure to laugh exactly in the right place.

Amid all this revelry, the stranger guest was very serious. He seemed sadder as the evening advanced, and, strange as it may appear, even the Baron's jokes seemed only to render him the more melancholy. At times he was lost in thought, and at times his restless eye showed a mind ill at ease. His conversations with the bride became more and more earnest and mysterious. She became uneasy and began to tremble.

All this could not escape the notice of the company. Their gaiety was chilled by the mysterious sadness of the bridegroom. Whispers and glances were exchanged, accompanied by shrugs and shakes of the head. The song and laughter grew less and less frequent. There were dreary pauses in the conversation, which were at length succeeded by wild tales and supernatural legends. One dismal story produced another still more dismal, and the Baron nearly frightened some of the ladies into hysterics with the history of the goblin horseman that carried away the fair Leonora, a dreadful but true story which has since been put into excellent verse and is read and believed by all the world.

The bridegroom listened to this tale with profound attention. He kept his eyes steadily fixed on the Baron, and as the story drew to a close, began gradually to rise from his seat, growing taller and taller, until he seemed almost to tower into a giant. The moment the tale was finished, he heaved a deep sigh and took a solemn farewell of the company. They were all amazed. The Baron was perfectly thunderstruck.

"What! Going to leave the castle at midnight? Why, everything is ready for you if you wish to retire."

The stranger shook his head mournfully, and mysteriously. "I must lay my head in a different chamber tonight!" he said.

There was something in this reply and the tone in which it was uttered that made the Baron's heart sink, but he repeated his hospitable offers.

The stranger shook his head silently at every one, and waving his farewell to the company, stalked slowly out of the hall. The maiden aunts were absolutely petrified—the bride hung her head and a tear stole to her eye.

The Baron followed the stranger to the great court of the castle, where the black charger stood pawing the earth and snorting with impatience. When they had reached the dimly lighted portal the stranger paused and addressed the Baron in a hollow voice.

"Now that we are alone," said he, "I will tell you the reason of my going. I have a solemn engagement—"

"Why," said the Baron, "can't you send someone in your place?"

TWO LADIES FAINTED OUTRIGHT.

"I must attend in person–I must go to Wurtzburg cathedral–"

"Aye," said the Baron, plucking up spirit, "but not until tomorrow–tomorrow you shall take your bride there."

"No! No!" replied the stranger, with great solemnity, "My engagement is with no bride. The worms! The worms expect me! I am a dead man–I have been slain by robbers–my body lies at Wurtzburg. At midnight I am to be buried–the grave is waiting for me–I must keep my appointment!"

He sprang on his black charger, dashed over the drawbridge, and the clattering of his horse's hoofs was lost in the whistling of the night wind.

The Baron returned to the hall in the utmost alarm and related what had passed. Two ladies fainted outright, others sickened at the idea of having dined with a specter. It was the opinion of some that this might be the wild huntsman famous in German legend. Some talked of other supernatural beings, with which the good people of Germany have been troubled since the beginning of time. Someone even suggested that it might have been a way for the young cavalier to avoid marriage, and that the very gloominess of his whim seemed to suit such a melancholy person.

But, whatever doubts were entertained, they were completely put to an end by the arrival, the next day, of news confirming the young Count's murder, and his burial in Wurtzburg cathedral.

The dismay at the castle may well be imagined. The Baron shut himself up in his chamber. The guests who had come to rejoice with him could not think of abandoning him in his distress. They wandered about the courts, or collected in groups in the hall, shaking their heads and shrugging their shoulders at the troubles of so good a man. They sat longer than ever at the table, and ate and drank more than ever, in order to keep up their spirits. But the situation of the widowed bride was the most pitiful. To have lost a husband before she had even embraced him—and such a husband! If the specter could be so gracious and noble, what must have been the living man! She filled the house with sorrow.

On the night of the second day of her widowhood she retired to her chamber, accompanied by one of her aunts, who insisted on sleeping with her. The aunt, who was one of the best tellers of ghost stories in all Germany, had just been retelling one of her longest, and had fallen asleep in the very midst of it.

The chamber overlooked a small garden. The niece lay gazing at the beams of the rising moon, as they trembled on the leaves of an aspen tree before the window. The castle clock had just tolled midnight when a soft strain of music stole up from the garden. She rose hastily from her bed, and stepped lightly to the window. A tall figure stood among the shadows of the trees. As it raised its head, a beam of moonlight fell upon the countenance. Heaven and earth! She beheld the Specter Bridegroom! At that moment a loud shriek burst upon her ear. Her aunt, who had been awakened by the music and had followed her silently to the window, fell into her arms. When she looked again, the specter had disappeared.

The aunt now required the most soothing, for she was perfectly beside herself with terror. As to the young lady, there was something endearing even in the ghost of her lover. The aunt declared she would never sleep in that chamber again.

The niece, for once, was stubborn, and declared that she would sleep in no other. As a result, she had to sleep alone, but she drew a promise from her aunt not to relate the story of the specter, in case she should be denied the only melancholy pleasure left her on earth that of inhabiting the chamber over which the guardian shadow of her lover kept its nightly vigils.

How long the good old lady would have observed this

A TALL FIGURE STOOD IN THE SHADOWS.

promise is uncertain, for she dearly loved to talk of the marvelous, and there is a triumph in being the first to tell a frightful story. It is, however, still quoted in the neighborhood as a memorable instance of female secrecy that she had kept it to herself for a whole week, when she was suddenly freed from all further restraint, by news brought to the breakfast table one morning that the young lady was not to be found. Her room was empty–the bed had not been slept in–the window was open, and the bird had flown!

The news was received with astonishment. Even the poor relations paused for a moment from the meal when the aunt, who had at first been struck speechless, wrung her hands and shrieked out, "The goblin! The goblin! She's carried away by the goblin!"

In a few words, she related the fearful scene of the garden, and concluded that the specter must have carried off his bride. Two of the servants supported the opinion, for they had heard the clattering of a horse's hoofs down the mountain about midnight, and had no doubt that it was the specter on his black charger, bearing her away to the tomb.

What a sad situation was that of the poor Baron! What a heartrending dilemma for a fond father and a member of the great family of Katzenellenbogen! His only daughter had either been taken to the grave, or he was to have some demon for a son-in-law, and perhaps a troop of goblin grandchildren. As usual, he was completely bewildered, and all the castle was in an uproar. The men were ordered to scour every road, path, and glen of the Odenwald on horseback. The Baron himself had just put on his boots and picked up his sword, and was about to mount his horse, when a new sight appeared. A lady and a cavalier approached the castle on horseback. When they reached the gate, the lady sprang from her horse, and falling at the Baron's feet, embraced his knees. It was his lost daughter and her companion, the Specter Bridegroom! The Baron was astounded. He looked at his daughter, then at the specter, in amazement. The ghost was wonderfully improved in his appearance since his visit to the world of spirits. His dress was splendid and he was no longer pale and melancholy. His face was flushed with the glow of youth and his dark eyes were filled with joy.

The mystery was soon cleared up. The cavalier (for in truth, as you must have known all the while, he was no goblin) announced himself as Sir Herman Von Starkenfaust. He related his adventure with the young Count. He told how he had hastened to the castle to deliver the unwelcome tidings, but that the eloquence of the Baron had interrupted him in every attempt to tell his tale. The sight of the bride had completely captivated him, and he allowed the mistake to continue so that he could pass a few hours near her. He didn't know how he could leave until the Baron's goblin stories had sug-

IT WAS HIS LOST DAUGHTER AND HER COMPANION—
THE SPECTER BRIDEGROOM!

gested his unusual exit. Fearing the hostility of the family because of old feuds, he had haunted the garden beneath the young lady's window and had managed to woo, then wed her.

Under any other circumstances, the Baron would have been inflexible, for he was proud of his authority and stubborn in all family feuds, but he loved his daughter. He had cried over her as lost, and he rejoiced to find her still alive. Though her husband was from the wrong family, at least he was not a goblin. It bothered the Baron that the knight played a joke on him, pretending to be a dead man, but several old friends who had fought in wars assured him that every strategy was excusable in love, and that the cavalier was entitled to special privilege, having been a soldier himself.

Matters, therefore, were happily arranged. The Baron pardoned the young couple on the spot. The revels at the castle were resumed. The poor relations overwhelmed this new member of the family with loving kindness. He was so gallant, so generous, so rich. The aunts, it is true, were somewhat shocked that their system of strict seclusion should turn out in such a way, but blamed themselves for not putting bars on the windows. One aunt was particularly embarrassed at having her marvelous story ruined, and that the only specter she had ever seen should turn out to be a fake, but the niece seemed perfectly happy that he turned out to be real flesh and blood.

4

The Devil and Tom Walker

A few miles from Boston, Massachusetts, a deep inlet winds several miles into the interior from Charles Bay and comes to an end in a thickly wooded swamp. One side of this inlet is a beautiful dark grove. On the opposite side, the land rises abruptly from the water's edge into a high ridge on which grow a few scattered oaks of great age and immense size.

Under one of these gigantic trees, according to old stories, there was a great treasure buried by Captain Kidd the pirate. The money was brought in a boat secretly and at night to the foot of the hill. The elevation of the place permitted a good lookout to be kept, and the trees formed landmarks by which the place might easily be found again. The old stories add, moreover, that the devil presided at the hiding of the money and took it under his care. This, it is well known, he always does with buried treasure, particularly when it has been ill gotten. Be that as it may, Kidd never returned to recover his wealth because he was seized at Boston, sent to England, and hanged there for being a pirate.

About the year 1727, when earthquakes were common in New England and shook many tall sinners down upon their knees, there lived near this place a miserly fellow named Tom Walker. He had a wife as miserly as himself. They were so miserly that they even conspired to cheat each other. Whatever the woman could lay hands on she hid away. A hen could not cackle but she was on the alert to secure the new laid egg. Her husband was continually prying about to find her secret hoards, and many and fierce were the conflicts that took place about what ought to have been common property.

They lived in a forlorn-looking house that stood alone and had an air of starvation. A few straggling trees grew near it; no smoke ever curled from its chimney; no traveller stopped at its door. A miserable horse, whose ribs were as plain to see as the bars of a grill, stalked about a field where a thin carpet of moss tantalized his hunger. Sometimes he would lean his head over the fence, look sadly at the passerby, and seem to ask deliverance from this famine.

The house and its inmates had altogether a bad name. Tom's wife was a nagging woman with a fierce temper, a loud tongue, and a strong arm. Her voice was often heard in wordy warfare with her husband, and his face sometimes showed signs that their conflicts were not confined to words. No one ventured, however, to interfere between them.

One day Tom Walker took what he considered a shortcut home through the swamp. Like most shortcuts, it was an ill-chosen route. The swamp was thickly grown with great gloomy pines and hemlocks, some of them ninety feet high, which made it dark at noonday. It was full of pits and quagmires, partly covered with weeds and mosses, where the green surface often betrayed the traveller into a gulf of black, smothering mud. There were also dark and stagnant pools, where the tadpole, the bull frog, and the water snake lived, where the trunks of pines and hemlocks lay half drowned, half rotting, looking like alligators sleeping in the mire.

Tom had been picking his way cautiously through this treacherous forest, stepping from tuft to tuft of rushes and roots which gave precarious footholds, or pacing carefully, like a cat along the fallen trunks of trees. He was startled now and then by the sudden screaming of the **bittern,** or the quacking of a

BITTERN
A wading bird sometimes called a thunder pumper because of its booming cry.

wild duck, rising on the wing from some solitary pool. At length he arrived at a piece of firm ground, which ran out like a peninsula deep into the swamp. It had been one of the strongholds of the Indians during their wars with the first colonists. Here they had thrown up a kind of fort which they had used as a place of refuge for their squaws and children. Nothing remained of the old Indian fort but a few mounds gradually sinking to the level of the surrounding earth, and already overgrown in part by oaks and other forest trees.

It was late in the dusk of evening when Tom Walker reached the old fort, and he paused there to rest. Anyone else would have felt unwilling to linger in this melancholy place, for most people had a bad opinion of it. There were stories handed down from the time of the Indian wars that the savages made sacrifices to the evil spirit here. Tom Walker, however, was not a man to be troubled with such fears.

He rested for some time on the trunk of a fallen hemlock, listening to the cry of the tree toad and poking with his walking staff into a mound of black mould at his feet. As he turned up the soil, his staff struck against something hard. He raked it out and lo! a skull with a rusted Indian tomahawk buried deep in it lay before him. It was a dreary memento of the fierce struggle that had taken place in this last foothold of the Indian warriors.

"Humph!" said Tom Walker, as he gave the skull a kick to shake the dirt from it.

"Let that skull alone!" said a gruff voice.

Tom lifted up his eyes and beheld a great black figure seated directly opposite him on the stump of a tree. Tom was exceedingly surprised, having neither seen nor heard anyone approach, and he was still more perplexed on observing, as well as the gathering gloom would permit, that the stranger's face was neither black nor copper color, but dingy with soot, as if he toiled among fires and forges. He had a shock of coarse black hair that stood out from his head in all directions, and he carried an axe on his shoulder.

He scowled at Tom with a pair of great red eyes.

"What are you doing on my grounds?" said the devil with a hoarse, growling voice.

"Your grounds?" said Tom, with a sneer. "No more your grounds than mine. They belong to Deacon Peabody."

"Deacon Peabody will be damned if he does not look more to his own sins and less to those of his neighbors," said the stranger. "Look yonder and see how Deacon Peabody is faring."

Tom looked in the direction that the stranger pointed, and beheld one of the great trees, flourishing on the outside, but rotten at the core, and saw that it had been nearly chopped through so that the first high wind was likely to blow it down. On the bark of the tree was carved the name of Deacon Peabody, a man who had become wealthy by driving shrewd bargains with the Indians. He now looked round and found most of the tall trees marked with the name of some great man of the colony. The one on which he had been seated, and which had evidently just been hewn down, bore the name of Crowninshield, and he recollected a mighty rich man of that name who made a vulgar display of wealth, which it was whispered he had gotten by **buccaneering**.

"He's just ready for burning!" said the devil, with a growl of triumph. "You see I have a good stock of firewood for winter."

"But what right have you," said Tom, "to cut down Deacon Peabody's timber?"

"The right of prior claim," said the other. "This woodland belonged to me long before one of your white-faced race put foot upon the soil."

BUCCANEERING
Piracy.

"And pray, who are you, if I may be so bold?" said Tom.

"Oh, I go by various names. I am the Wild Huntsman in some countries, the Black Miner in others. In this neighborhood I am known by the name of the Black Woodsman.

The Indians made this spot sacred to me, and they now and then roasted a white man in sacrifice. Since the red men have been exterminated by you white savages, I amuse myself by presiding at the persecutions of **Quakers** and **Anabaptists** . I am the great patron of slave dealers and the grand master of the **Salem witches**."

One would think that to meet with such a singular personage in this wild, lonely place would have shaken any man's nerves. But Tom was a hard-minded fellow, and he had lived so long with a scolding wife that he did not even fear the devil.

QUAKERS AND ANABAPTISTS
Though many people came to America from Europe to gain religious freedom, some religious groups such as Quakers and Anabaptists, who refused to fight in wars, were often harassed in the colonies.

SALEM WITCHES
In 1692, 20 so-called witches were tried and executed in Salem, Massachusetts.

They had a long and earnest conversation together, as Tom returned home. The devil told him of great sums of money buried by Captain Kidd the pirate, under the oak trees on the high ridge not far from the swamp. All these were under his command and protected by his power, so that none could find them but those in his favor. These he offered to place within Tom Walker's reach, but only under certain conditions. What these conditions were Tom never disclosed. They must have been very hard, for he required time to think of them, and he was not a man to hesitate where money was in view. When they had reached the edge of the swamp the stranger paused.

"What proof have I that all you have been telling me is true?" said Tom.

"There is my signature," said the black man, pressing his finger on Tom's forehead. So saying, he turned off among the thickets of the swamp, and seemed, as Tom said, to go down, down, down, into the earth, until nothing but his head and shoulders could be seen, and so on until he totally disappeared.

When Tom reached home he found a black fingerprint burned into his forehead, which nothing could remove.

The first news his wife had to tell him was of the sudden death of Absalom Crowninshield, the rich buccaneer. Tom recollected the tree which his black friend had just hewn down, and which was ready for burning. "Let him roast," said Tom, "Who cares!" He now felt convinced that all he had heard and seen was no illusion.

He was not prone to let his wife into his confidence, but as this was an uneasy secret, he shared it with her. All her greed was awakened at the mention of hidden gold, and she urged her husband to consent to the black man's terms and secure what would make them wealthy for life. Although Tom might have felt willing to sell himself to the devil, he was determined not to do so to please his wife. So he flatly refused out of the mere spirit of contradiction. Many and bitter were the quarrels they had on the subject, but the more she talked, the more resolute was Tom not to be damned to please her. At length she decided to drive the bargain on her own account, and if she succeeded, to keep all the gain to herself.

Being of the same fearless temper as her husband, she set off for the old Indian fort towards the close of a summer day. When she came back after many hours she was reserved and sullen in her replies. She spoke something of a black man whom she had met about twilight, chopping at the root of a tall tree. He was sulky, however, and would not come to terms. She was to bring him something, but what it was she wouldn't say.

The next evening she set off again for the swamp with her apron heavily laden. Tom waited and waited for her, but in vain. Midnight came, but she did not make her appearance. Morning, noon, and night returned, but still she did not come. Tom now grew uneasy for her safety, especially as he found she had carried off in her apron the silver teapot and spoons and everything of value she could carry. She was never heard of again.

Her real fate nobody knows. Some said that she lost her way among the tangled mazes of the swamp and sank into some pit. Others, more uncharitable, hinted that she had taken the household booty and run away. Some others asserted that the tempter had lured her into a quagmire. It was said a great black figure with an axe on his shoulder was seen late that very evening coming out of the swamp, carrying a bundle tied in an apron.

Tom Walker grew so anxious about the fate of his wife and his property that he set out to seek them both at the Indian fort. During a long summer afternoon he searched about the gloomy place, and called his wife repeatedly, but she was nowhere to be heard. The bittern alone responded to his voice, as it flew screaming by, and the bullfrog croaked dolefully from a neighboring pool. At length, just in the brown hour of twilight, when the owls began to hoot and the bats to flit about, his attention was attracted by the clamor of crows hovering about a cypress tree. He looked up and saw a bundle tied in an apron hanging in the branches of the tree, with a great vulture perched nearby, as if keeping watch upon it. He leaped with joy, for he recognized his wife's apron and supposed it to contain the household valuables.

"Let us get hold of the property," said he, to himself, "and we will do without the woman."

As he scrambled up the tree the vulture spread its wide wings and sailed off screaming into the deep shadows of the forest. Tom seized the checked apron, but found nothing but a heart and liver tied up in it.

Such, according to the most authentic old story, was all that was to be found of Tom's wife. She had probably tried to deal with the devil as she had been used to dealing with her husband. Though a female scold is generally considered a match for the devil, in this instance she appears to have had the worst of it. She must have given a good fight, however, for it is said Tom noticed many prints of cloven feet deeply stamped around the tree, and found handfuls of hair that looked as if they had been plucked from the coarse black shock of the woodsman. "Egad," said Tom to himself, "He must have had a tough time of it!"

Tom consoled himself for the loss of his property with the loss of his wife, for he was a man of fortitude. He even felt something like gratitude towards the black woodsman, who he considered had done him a kindness. He sought, therefore, to cultivate a further acquaintance with him, but for some time without success. Whatever people may think, the devil is not always easy to call upon. He knows how to play his cards when pretty sure of his game.

At length, it is said, when delay had whetted Tom's eagerness to the quick and prepared him to agree to anything to gain the promised treasure, he met the devil one evening in his usual woodman dress, with his axe on his shoulder, sauntering along the edge of the swamp and humming a tune. He received Tom's advances with indifference and went on humming his tune.

By degrees, however, Tom brought him to business, and they began to haggle about the terms on which the former was to have the pirate's treasure. There was one condition which need not be mentioned, being generally understood in **all cases where the devil grants favors,** but there were others about which, though of less importance, he was inflexibly obstinate. He insisted that the money should be employed in his service. He proposed, therefore, that Tom should fit out a slave ship. This, however, Tom resolutely refused. He knew he was already bad enough as he was. The devil himself could not tempt him to become a slave dealer.

Finding Tom so squeamish on this point, he did not insist upon it, but proposed instead that he should become a **usurer.** The devil looked upon such people as his own.

To this Tom made no objections, for it was just to his taste.

ALL CASES WHERE THE DEVIL GRANTS FAVORS
A person who accepts a favor from the devil must give the devil his soul in return.

"You shall open a broker's shop in Boston next month," said the devil.

"I'll do it tomorrow, if you wish," said Tom Walker.

"You shall lend money at two percent a month."

"Egad, I'll charge four!" replied Tom Walker.

"You shall foreclose **mortgages**, drive the merchant to bankruptcy–"

"I'll drive him to the devil," cried Tom Walker, eagerly.

USURER
Someone who loans money at rates so high that people have trouble ever paying it back.

MORTGAGES
A loan on property in which the borrower agrees to give up the property if he does not make the payments on the loan. Foreclosure is when the lender takes the property.

"You are the usurer for my money!" said the devil, with delight. "When will you want the cash?"

"This very night."

"Done!" said the devil.

"Done!" said Tom Walker. So they shook hands and struck a bargain.

A few days' time saw Tom Walker seated behind his desk in a counting house in Boston. His reputation for a man who would lend money out for a high fee soon spread. It was a time when paper money was particularly scarce and credit was common. There had been a rage for speculating. People had run mad with schemes for new settlements and building cities in the wilderness; land jobbers went about with maps of townships and **El Dorado**, lying nobody knew where, but which everybody was ready to purchase. In a word, the great speculating fever which breaks out every now and then in the country raged to an alarming degree, and everybody was dreaming of making sudden fortunes from nothing. As usual, the fever subsided. The dream had gone off, and the imaginary fortunes with it. The whole country was in "hard times."

EL DORADO A place with many riches, from the Spanish for "covered in gold."

At this time of public distress, Tom Walker set up as a usurer in Boston. His door was soon thronged by customers. The needy and the adventurous, the gambling speculator, the dreaming land jobber, the thriftless tradesman, the merchant with cracked credit, in short, everyone driven to raise money by desperate means and desperate sacrifices hurried to Tom Walker.

Thus Tom was the universal friend of the needy, and he acted like a "friend in need"–that is to say, he always demanded good pay and good security. The more distressed the applicant, the harder Tom's terms. He accumulated bonds and mortgages. He gradually squeezed more and more money from his customers and sent them dry as a sponge from his door.

In this way he became a rich and mighty man. He built himself a vast house, out of ostentation, but left the greater part of it unfinished and unfurnished out of stinginess. He even set up a carriage, though he nearly starved the horses which drew it; and as the ungreased wheels groaned and screeched on the axle trees, you would have thought you heard the souls of the poor debtors he was squeezing.

As Tom grew old, however, he grew thoughtful. Having secured the good things of this world, he began to feel anxious about those of the next. He thought with regret on the bargain he had made with the devil and set his wits to work to cheat him out of the conditions. He became, therefore, all of a sudden, a violent churchgoer. He prayed loudly as if heaven were to be taken by force of lungs. Indeed, one might always tell when he had sinned most during the week, by the clamor of his Sunday devotion. The quiet Christians who had been modestly and steadfastly making their way toward heaven were struck at seeing themselves so suddenly overtaken by this new convert. Tom was as rigid in religious as in money matters. He was a stern supervisor and critic of his neighbors and seemed to think every sin in their account became a credit on his own side of the page. He even talked of renewing the persecution of

Quakers and Anabaptists. In a word, Tom's zeal became as notorious as his riches.

Still, in spite of all this strenuous attention to forms, Tom had a dread that the devil, after all, would have his due. So that he might not be taken by surprise, therefore, he carried a small Bible in his coat pocket. He also had a large one on his counting house desk, and would frequently be found reading it when people called on business. On such occasions, he would lay his green spectacles in the book to mark the place, while he turned round to take advantage of another customer.

Some say that Tom grew a little crack-brained in his old days, and that when he thought that his end was approaching, he had his horse new shod, saddled and bridled, and buried with his feet uppermost. Tom supposed that on the last day the world would be turned upside down, in which case he should find his horse standing ready for mounting, and he was determined at the worst to give his old friend a run for it. This, however, is probably just an old wives' fable. If he really did take such a precaution, it was totally unnecessary, at least so says the authentic old legend which gives the end of his story in the following manner.

One hot afternoon in the **dog days**, just as a terrible black thunderstorm was coming up, Tom sat in his counting house in his white linen cap and India silk morning gown. He was on the point of foreclosing a mortgage, by which he would complete the ruin of an unlucky land speculator for whom he had professed the greatest friendship. The poor man begged him for a few more months to pay off his debt. Tom had grown irritated and refused another day.

"My family will be ruined," said the man. "Charity begins at home," replied Tom, "I must take care of myself in these hard times."

"You have made so much money out of me," said the speculator.

Tom lost his patience—"The devil take me," said he, "if I have made a penny!"

Just then there were three loud knocks at the street door. Tom stepped out to see who was there. The devil was holding a black horse which neighed and stamped with impatience.

"Tom, you're come for!" said the devil, gruffly. Tom shrunk back, but too late. He had left his little Bible at the bottom of his coat pocket, and his big Bible on the desk was buried under the mortgage he was about to foreclose. Never

THE DOG · Sirius

DOG DAYS
The hottest weeks of the year in July and August, so named because they coincide with the rising of the Dog Star, Sirius, in the heavens.

was a sinner taken more unawares. The devil whisked him like a child into the saddle, gave the horse a lash, and away he galloped with Tom on his back, in the midst of a thunderstorm. The clerks stuck their pens behind their ears and stared after him from the windows. Away went Tom Walker, dashing down the streets, his white cap bobbing up and down, his morning gown fluttering in the wind, and his steed striking fire out of the pavement at every bound. When the clerks turned to look for the devil, he had disappeared.

Tom Walker never returned to foreclose the mortgage. A countryman who lived on the border of the swamp reported that in the height of the thunderstorm he had heard a great clattering of hoofs and a howling down the road, and running to the window caught sight of a figure such as I have described on a horse that galloped like mad across the fields, over the hills and down into the black hemlock swamp toward the old Indian fort. Shortly after that a thunderbolt falling in that direction seemed to set the whole forest in a blaze.

The good people of Boston shook their heads and shrugged their shoulders, but had been so much accustomed to witches and goblins and tricks of the devil in all kinds of shapes from the first settlement of the colony, that they were not so much horror struck as might have been expected. Trustees were appointed to take charge of Tom's effects. There was nothing, however, to administer upon. On searching his coffers, they found all his bonds and mortgages reduced to cinders. In place of gold and silver his iron chest was filled with chips and shavings. Two skeletons lay in his stable instead of his half-starved horses, and the very next day his great house burned to the ground.

Such was the end of Tom Walker and his ill-gotten wealth. Let all money brokers take this story to heart. The truth of it is not to be doubted. The very hole under the oak trees whence he dug Kidd's money is to be seen to this day, and the neighboring swamp and old Indian fort are often haunted on stormy nights by a figure on horseback, in a morning gown and white cap.

Washington Irving

WASHINGTON IRVING (1783-1859) WAS THE FIRST American author who earned his living by writing. He was born in New York City, the youngest of eleven children. His father, an immigrant from Scotland who prospered as a hardware merchant, was stern and aloof, but his mother spoiled him. When he was very little, President George Washington, for whom he was named, once patted him on the head.

He daydreamed a lot as a boy and was a lazy student. His education would have been poor, if not for the fact that he loved to read so much. As he grew older he worked in one brother's hardware business and in another brother's law firm, but he found both jobs boring. He got his start as a writer, using a false name, in another brother's newspaper. His arti-

New York
Jan. 1851

Washington Irving

Sunnyside Dec 15th 1851

cles poked fun at New York society, which in his day had the traits of small town life.

At family expense he travelled in Europe for two years and his adventures included being on a boat captured by pirates. Home again in 1809, he published *A History of New York,* giving the author's name as Diedrich Knickerbocker, and it became very popular. Though it pretends to be serious and scholarly, it is a comic account of the state's settlement by the Dutch and its politics. He advertised the book by putting up notices around town saying that the scholar Diedrich Knickerbocker had disappeared, but an unknown manuscript of his had been found.

Well-liked in society for his friendly temper and polished manners, Irving spent the next ten years idly following fashion and politics. During the War of 1812, he served as a colonel in the New York militia. During this period, his fiancee, Matilda Hoffman, died of tuberculosis. His grief was great, but as time went on he grew attached to the freedoms of bachelorhood and he never married.

He went to Liverpool, England, in 1815 to run the family's business there, but by 1818 their firm was bankrupt. Pressed by necessity and encouraged by Sir Walter Scott's confidence in him, Irving went from dillydallying to diligence, determined to earn a living with his pen.

A year later, *The Sketch Book* appeared, containing the first true American short stories, including "The Legend of Sleepy Hollow" and "Rip Van Winkle." He continued to write, but also accepted a diplomatic post in Spain, living four years in the Alhambra, the dazzling citadel of Spain's Moorish kings. His subjects switched to history and biography, which he found easier than inventing stories. Using Spanish archives, he wrote *A History of the Life and Voyages of Christopher Columbus* and *A Chronicle of the Conquest of Grenada.*

By the time he returned to the United States in 1832, after an absence of seventeen years, he was a national hero for having won acceptance in European literary circles and having friends such as Charles Dickens. In search of new subjects he toured the frontier and wrote *A Tour of the Prairies* and *Astoria*, the story of the American trading post on the Columbia River.

His reputation among Europeans led to his being named ambassador to Spain in 1842. He dutifully spent the next four years amidst the treachery and intrigue of the royal court. Later he turned down all public posts, including a nomination to Congress, an offer to be secretary of the Navy and an appeal to run for mayor of New York, because he preferred to write and to be at home.

He bought a small Dutch-built cottage near Tarrytown, New York, in 1833. First he called it The Roost,

SUNNYSIDE: IRVING'S HOME

the Dutch word for rest, and then he changed its name to Sunnyside. He added on to the house, entertained his literary friends, raised poultry, and puttered contentedly among his farm animals, including a favorite pig he named Fanny. He died at Sunnyside in 1859, shortly after finishing the project of his elderly years, *The Life of George Washington.*

He is remembered in history books as America's first professional man of letters, but he is appreciated now more for his clear, elegant style, which conveys his charming and generous personality.